SPACE CAPTAIN

ADELAIDE

SHADOWS OF THE FALLEN

ISBN: 978-0-9880932-6-3
WGA Library of Congress

Illustrated by Jackson Gee
Formatted by Firefly Designs

Disclaimer: This is a work of fiction. Names, characters,
events, locations and incidents either are the product of the
author's imagination or are used fictitiously. Any actual
resemblances to actual persons, living or dead, or locales are
entirely coincidental.

www.yvonnemysteries.com

A HUGE THANKS TO MY SISTER AND BROTHER FOR THEIR HELP WITH EDITING BEFORE I SENT OFF THE MANUSCRIPT AND TO MY BETA READERS FOR THEIR INPUT AND SUGGESTIONS. MY FAMILY HAS ALWAYS BEEN SUPPORTIVE, AND IT'S GREATLY APPRECIATED.

SPACE CAPTAIN ADELAIDE
A CRIME LORD'S DEBT
SHADOW OF THE FALLEN

THE KAILA PORTER SERIES
MURDER FROM BEYOND THE GRAVE
SWEETEST REVENGE
INCINERATED

SPACE CAPTAIN ADELAIDE ZEDLER
BORN IN 2075; 33 YEARS OLD

OCCUPATION: CAPTAIN IN EARTH'S MILITARY

PLANET: EARTH2
- *Earth has become very careful about preserving unsustainable resources*
- *She lives in the capital city, Transmont*
- *Hollow Peasant is her favorite watering hole*
- *Earth is part of the Multi-Species Accords*

PHYSICAL DESCRIPTION:
Red curly, shoulder-length hair; thin, straight, freckled nose; green eyes; small waist; large chest; 5'5" tall; communications unit attached to wrist (looks kind of like a large square watch); high muscle tone and definition; very pretty.

WEAPONS:
Blaster on each hip, knives in each boot and a smaller blaster on her thigh.

PERSONALITY/EMOTIONS:
Strong-willed, nerves of steel, fierce, feisty, sarcastic.

FAVOURITE FOOD AND DRINK:
Meat pastry from Gaeaf, Toph non-alcoholic beverage from Zartuth, garpel drink from Zartuth

Chapter 1

Adelaide tapped her foot on the console in front of her captain's chair, tugging on a strand of curly red hair as she brooded about her impending arrival on Earth. She'd made no plans to return to the main military base after her retirement.

Gil's stomps sounded on the bridge. "Captain." Giving a grunt, he lowered his slim frame into the chair. He was her only remaining family, even if their blood differed.

Her heart hurt imagining something happening to him. It almost kept her from begging him to join her crew in the coming days, but he was the only person she trusted to watch her back.

"Are we ready?" she asked.

"Yes. I'm going to miss this old girl." He patted the panel beside him.

"We'll have her back; this is just temporary." She glanced over, catching the doubt in Gil's eyes. But Adelaide refused to acknowledge his pessimism. No way would she want to fly the ZOO without him. Gil was her rock. Plus, he knew the ship like the back of his hand. After removing two of her father's cargo ships from the roster and running the ZOO with Gil, Adelaide realized what a gem he was. Her father's death wounded deep, and the fighting with her now-deceased brother over the transport company had only caused more distress. The decision to operate alone with Gil at the engines had been the best decision for her. The ZOO's small size made a two-man crew viable.

"Captain, we are entering Earth's orbit." ALICE's voice came through the comm. Advanced Logic Intelligent Command Environment—the brains of the ZOO—was capable of learning which was standard and developing a personality was an option available. Of course, that was the first option Adelaide clicked on after installation, ALICE was already showing signs of snarkiness.

An immense wall of metal slid into view, obscuring the planet. The three round segments seemed to stretch on forever. Docking ports, airlocks and antennas encrusted the central hull of the immense space station, five million tons of shining aluminium alloy, plexiglass and high-tech composites. Far above were the edges of the three habitation rings, speckled with navigation lights—man-made stars to guide myriad incoming travellers to their berths.

"Did you ever imagine Earth could construct something like this? And keep it going?" Her eyes never left the station.

"What, with the war and all the chaos afterward? It's a wonder we ever managed."

Adelaide glanced over to see a far away expression on Gil's face. "We'd never have done it without the Accords; we were decades from the tech."

Years ago, Earth couldn't wait to sign the Accords and become members of the Syndicate. With the defences offered, humans stood a chance against all the new species they were encountering during their forage into space. Every member shared information and provided military in times of need.

Gil nodded. "You know the odds of—"

Before Gil could finish Adelaide shook her head. "We're not talking doom and gloom before we even start. Get that out of your head right now." She glared at Gil.

With a grin, he held up his hands in surrender. "Fine. We're going to kick ass and take names."

"That's right, and I don't need any lip from you. Get us ready for re-entry."

Gil stood, saluting. "Yes, Captain. I'll be in engineering."

"Ass," Adelaide muttered under her breath as Gil's muscular form slowly walked away. For an older guy, he was still in great shape.

Adelaide frowned as she watched Gil stumble, a shaking hand pressed against the wall. Though he was getting up in years, the mid-sixties were nothing nowadays—a drop in the bucket with half his life to still live. But last time she'd been down in engineering, Gil seemed to have difficulties standing up. When Adelaide tried to assist, Gil pushed her away grumbling about her coddling him. Hopefully, he would pass their required physical from the military doctors.

"ALICE, inform the base of our arrival."

"Yes, Captain."

Adelaide pushed the necessary buttons in anticipation of their descent. The blackness of space merged with the blue of the thermosphere as the ZOO's engines slowed. They flew into white fluffy clouds, eventually breaking through above the base. The dome encompassing the base flickered, and an opening appeared at the top close to their position. Guiding the ship through, she noted nothing had changed since her last visit.

After touching down, Adelaide deboarded, leaving Gil to complete the docking checklist. She stopped a few feet away on the landing pad, lifting her grinning face to the sky. As a light breeze lifted the hair from her neck, she breathed deep, filling her lungs with the fresh earthy air, so much better than the recycled kind she was used to. A squadron of ships flew overhead, their engines blocking the noise from the surrounding ground traffic. The ships practiced maneuvers the military taught every pilot. A horn beeped; Adelaide jumped back as a truck drove past with the driver yelling in her direction. She glanced around; a vehicle was parked in every bay in the hanger. The airfield was jam-packed as well.

Clusters of military personnel dotted the area, their voices drifting towards her on the warm breeze.

"You seen the video?" one soldier asked his comrade as Adelaide strode passed.

4

"It looks like those damn Cradesions to me; I guess they're …"

Adelaide snuck a peek at the two as an involuntary shiver passed through her body. If that warlike race hadn't been destroyed, if they were reappearing—

Their voices faded as Adelaide turned the corner, walking into a large crowd.

"Excuse me, coming through," she said, using her elbows.

While surprise appeared on many faces, everyone moved out of her way.

"Who's that?" someone whispered.

"You don't know Captain Zedler?" another voice questioned, shock in their voice.

"Captain, wait. I want to shake your hand."

Sighing, she turned around.

"It's an honour to meet you. I was at the last battle with the Raykar. If you hadn't crashed your battleship into the enemy's vessels, we would have lost." The soldier seemed a little younger than her thirty-three years. He grabbed her outstretched hand, pumping it vigorously. Before she could escape, a few more replaced the first wanting to meet her.

Finally extracting herself, she rushed towards the general's office. It was over four years since the Raykar war; didn't people have better things to do then remember who she was? While her part in the war was her duty, it had been a privilege defending their species. Many soldiers should be distinguished from their fellow officers.

Adelaide stepped into the dragon's lair with a sigh, not sure if from relief or trepidation. Mrs. Turner made everyone nervous.

"Is General Williams in his office?" Adelaide asked, fiddling with the couple of curls escaping from her ponytail before she forced her body to remain still. She was a military captain for God's sake. How was it possible to still react this strongly? It amazed Adelaide that Dragon Lady hadn't retired from the service.

Mrs. Turner's thin lips curved slightly, Adelaide wasn't sure if she was attempting to smile or to grimace. Hopefully not the latter. All the older recruits knew to be leery of Mrs. Turner's grimace. During Adelaide's first year, her class had experienced the Turner glare, followed by gruelling laps around the base in the pouring rain then combat fighting. It was a great way to weed out the weak.

"He's waiting for you." Mrs. Turner gestured to the closed door. "Glad to see you, Adelaide."

Adelaide gawked at her. *Was that a real smile?* Adelaide thought as the dragon peered down at the monitor, her thinning white hair held in a tight bun. Couldn't have been. Adelaide shook her head, knocking on the general's door before entering.

"General." Adelaide saluted.

"At ease, Captain. I'm glad you're here. I've got a mission for you."

"Already?"

"Yes. I need you to take a squad for reconnaissance on Tikaani."

The planet sounded familiar, but Adelaide couldn't place it.

"Communications from Tikaani were cut off twenty days ago. From what we can gather, a very serious incident has occurred—on a planetary scale."

"Why haven't I heard anything? Something would have leaked if it were such a big deal."

"The Syndicate wants it kept quiet until the cause of radio silence has been established."

"Are other species sending soldiers? I heard the Syndicate was trying to recruit more species to sign the Accords."

"No. You're going to be the first. Multiple probes were launched, but all were destroyed soon after reaching the planet."

Adelaide leaned forward; her brows furrowed. "Why do you expect a different outcome if a scout ship arrives?"

"We have precautions in place. Besides, you are larger than a probe, and you have weapons."

"Didn't Tikaani rebuke the Accords? Why does the Syndicate care?" Adelaide asked. Though harsh, they didn't spend resources on non-members.

"Wasn't there a planet a few years back?" Adelaide tapped her chin. "Wadenic. They were devastated by earthquakes, floods, and fires the Syndicate refused to send help."

"They're afraid one of them will be targeted next if this is the Cradesions."

She lifted her eyebrows. "So, it's self interest rather than humanitarian."

The general scowled. "Don't repeat that outside of this room. You won't like the consequences."

She knew it was an offense to disparage the Syndicate. Overall, they were a great entity. But there was no such thing as perfect.

The general turned his monitor. "I have a video from the destruction of the city Kahoon."

"I've seen it."

"Just watch."

The screen showed what she assumed was the planet Janpar. One large, cubed metal station with two-gun ports and a couple of small docking bays floated in orbit. One minute it was there; the next, large pieces of debris were floating in space.

"What the hell!" she swore.

"Keep watching."

She glanced back to the screen, seeing the same scene that had been played throughout the galaxy except for large distortions streaking across the sky. Then massive craters exploded, engulfing the city Kahoon. Nothing was left standing. Two and a half million lives were wiped out in seconds. No chance of survival.

"Where did you get this?" she asked. "Are those distortions cloaked ships?"

"Classified. The experts believe so, but even close analysis cannot confirm anything."

"So why do they suspect Tikaani is the same?"

"Because the probes could not verify the location of the space station. We need confirmation what is happening to the planet. Before the probes were destroyed, a message was sent but nothing is received."

"How many will be on my team? I've recruited Gil from my crew." Adelaide frowned. She didn't want unknown baggage on a sensitive mission. Being in the military and captaining a ship, Adelaide had depended on a large crew to keep everyone safe. But since flying the ZOO, she'd had only Gil to rely on, and she'd grown used to it.

"He'll be an asset." The general nodded. Gil was well known in the military, fighting in WWIII as well as multiple battles since Earth became a space-faring species. "I have two more in mind."

After he typed something on his computer, her wrist comm beeped. When she pushed a button, the holodisplay showed files being uploaded.

"Those are the specs on the men. Read them over tonight and inform me by 0600. You are flying out tomorrow at 1700. A skeleton crew is already assigned."

Adelaide's brow raised though she consciously refrained from grimacing. What did they need a crew for on a reconnaissance mission?

"They have been trained on this vessel and will be essential if you experience combat."

She could use all the advantages possible. Maybe she'd been alone too long. Just her and Gil all those years.

"Mrs. Turner will send you all their service records." The general rapped his knuckles against the desktop.

"Okay."

"You and Lieutenant Gil will have to learn the ship's systems on route. Any problems?"

"No sir. I want Gil in charge of engineering."

"I anticipated the request. It has already been put into the works as long as he passes the medical."

Adelaide flinched, hoping he did. "What ship are we taking?"

"We have a new ship with cloaking capabilities and a prototype internal jump gate."

Adelaide grinned in delight. She'd heard rumours of new construction but didn't want to get her hopes up. "Was the Syndicate able to use Raykar tech?"

The general nodded.

"And this jump gate works?" she asked, narrowing her eyes. She had no plans to be going on a suicide mission.

"From the test trials, yes."

"Meaning?" Adelaide kept voice even.

"They've tested twice before. Both trials had issues with overheating. We didn't plan to implement the jump gate until it was ready, but you may need the option depending on what you discover at Tikaani. Our scientists are working on the solution; we don't want to leave you defenceless if you face a large force there. This equipment is a need-to-know basis."

"Understood. What's her name?"

He cocked his head. "Her?"

"If the ship's as fancy as you say, it must be a female." Adelaide laughed, unable to contain her excitement. Captaining a new ship might make coming back worth it.

"Its name is the Clandestine." He smirked. "Consider it whatever gender you want."

"If this miniature jump gate works, it will be monumental. It could also devastate many planets' economies if they no longer receive the exorbitant fees from other ships using their jump gates."

"This is needed. Not many gates exist. It will be years before many can incorporate this technology with their ships. Even then, it's expensive technology, so the jump gates defended by the Syndicate members will still be utilized."

Other species could pay the planet an exorbitant fee to use the gate or try entering by force. Only a few were ever able to pass through to cause problems in other parts of the galaxy.

"We'll send you our intel regarding Tikaani." The general nodded toward Adelaide's wrist. "I want you to report to the health facility now for a comms and translator upgrade, along with your physical."

Adelaide twisted her lips. Having them upgraded hurt. Her wrist twinged with the phantom pain of the last connection. "What's wrong with my current model?"

"I assume you haven't upgraded since leaving the military?"

"No, I haven't found it necessary."

"With this new ship, you need the updated comms. As well, the interpretation chip has been outfitted with what little language is known of the Cradesions and more of the outlying planets."

Adelaide rubbed behind her left ear feeling the interpretation chip implanted years ago. Changing the chip would sever her link to ALICE, putting one more speck of doubt into her mind. There would be no more dry voice talking her down from a ledge she had crawled onto. Giving stats on other species and locations the ship encountered.

Nodding, Adelaide studied her holodisplay. "Do we have enough data for the Cradesion language? I thought no one who would have an inkling of the Cradesion language survived the war with them."

"You're correct, but we found a few documents. It won't be enough yet to assist with their language at the beginning. But if you can provide the chip with more data, it should be able to start interpretating."

"Okay, let's hope it learns fast. I'll review the stats of the crew and let you know."

"Dismissed. And Captain, I expect frequent reports."

"Yes sir." Adelaide saluted before leaving.

Exiting the building, Adelaide glanced at the hovering dark clouds. The moisture felt cool against her warm skin. The air was dry on Earth compared to Earth2, which she called home. After the devastation of plant life and the rebuilding, revitalization of the planet never regained the same water levels.

On Earth2, plants and water covered eighty-five percent of the planet. Moisture was constantly in the air. Many people from Earth had difficulties adapting to the change especially with breathing.

Adelaide waved down a transport for a lift to the health facility. Might as well get it over with. During the trip across the base, Adelaide informed ALICE of the subsequent surgery and the impending silence.

"Are you sure it is necessary, Captain?" ALICE inquired.

"I've been told it is in order to interface with the new ship."

"What new ship?" ALICE demanded.

"The military developed a new advanced ship. I've scanned some of the specs; it seems impressive."

During the following pause, Adelaide wondered if ALICE signed off. "ALICE?"

"Once your mission is completed, you will initiate our interface."

"Yes. I will contact you when we arrive. Captain, out."

*   *   *

When Adelaide stepped into the medical building, Dr. Moniker greeted her. "Adelaide, I was expecting you."

"You're waiting for me at the door?" she asked, surprised.

"Yes. I didn't want you changing your mind." He grinned, motioning her to follow him to the back.

Large oval lights hung from the vaulted ceilings, casting a glare off the sterile white walls onto the cement floors. Adelaide wrinkled her nose as the sharp reek of chemicals permeated the room, burning the little hairs in her nostrils. A hint of lemon did nothing to mask the other smells.

Dr. Moniker glanced back at her frozen form. "Hurry up. I don't have all day."

Adelaide strode to catch up before the travel tube closed. They were shot up the four floors and spit out onto a large platform.

He led her into a room, where he motioned towards a small platform, not comfortable enough to be a bed. Adelaide hopped up waiting expectantly.

"Alright, give me your wrist. You know how this procedure works?" he asked.

"Oh, ya think?" She grimaced, not excited to have the wires pulled from her body.

Adelaide shoved out her wrist. "Get to it, doc."

"I want you to lie down so I can strap you in place."

Once she was prone, he grabbed straps from either side of the bed, attaching them across her chest and legs, snapping her forearm in a cuff. Though she tried to hold still, her body tensed with expectation.

"How do you know it hasn't connected to my chip?" she demanded, scrutinizing Dr. Moniker's every move. The personal chip was embedded in a person's hand. It was connected to their brain, removing it was lethal. All private information was stored there. Banking information, employment status, residence etc. Information no one wanted available. Though extremely rare, the personal chip could merge with another implant, like her comm.

"Well, I don't yet. But I have this." He held up his tablet, activating a holodisplay. As he slid the machine along her arm to her fingertips, Adelaide's internal musculature came into view. "This shows there is no connecting pieces, natural or machine." Dr. Moniker pointed to the area on the display.

She gave a sigh of relief. One less thing to worry about.

"I'm attaching a pain strip. You shouldn't feel anything after. Just yell if you do." Eyes twinkling, he turned away for a moment.

"Thanks, doc. I'll be sure to scream loudly for your benefit." She glared at his back. When he returned, she took a deep breath as he pressed the strip to her arm.

After grabbing a pointy tool, he used it to scan over her hand, then poked her.

"Ow!" she screamed.

He jumped back. "I'm sorry."

Adelaide laughed at his expression "Gotcha."

If looks could kill, it was a good thing she was at the hospital already.

Poking her again, he watched her face for a reaction.

"Nothing," she said.

"Let's get started, then." With a scalpel, he sliced a thin cut above the comm unit. Next, he picked a minuscule tool from the tray inserting it into the cut. Watching the monitor, he navigated towards the living tentacles protruding from the comm which were attached to her veins and muscles. It took awhile to cut all the connections before making an incision under the unit so it could be removed.

"This is a computer—why can't you just upgrade the software?"

"Because the material on this model is obsolete, they've had issues with some malfunctioning. The type of hardware used in this model can't process the new ships' systems."

Adelaide stared in horror at her wrist. "What do you mean malfunction?" she demanded.

He sighed. "Some have caught on fire."

It was a good thing she was strapped in because Adelaide couldn't stop the twitch. She glared at the offending machinery as he slowly pulled it from her wrist, the tentacles followed leaving little holes in her skin.

After dropping it into a bin close by, he grabbed the shiny new black replacement comm, holding it up for her inspection. No matter how many times she saw the moving tentacles, they still freaked her out. Having something living and foreign inserted into her body seemed wrong. In his other hand, he held the special tool needed to insert the new unit.

Watching the things pushed into her wrist and feeling the little tingles as they moved through her body gave Adelaide the shivers.

"Finished. Let's examine your translator chip."

Adelaide shook her head. "It should be fine."

"Don't be a baby." He rolled his eyes. "You know, Gil didn't move a muscle."

She muttered under her breath. At least she knew Gil must have passed the physical—they wouldn't have given him upgrades otherwise.

"Why wasn't I given my physical first?" she asked, turning her head to allow him access to the chip.

"I know you, my dear. You would have tried to talk your way out of the upgrades. This way, it's done. Besides, with you your physical is only a formality."

He glanced professionally down her five-foot-five frame. The muscle definition she worked so hard for showed through her tight clothing. Being the owner and captain of the cargo ship, she was required to submit to a yearly checkup with the med bot on board.

"Are you required to remove the chip as well?" she asked. It was connected directly to their brain; she didn't want someone fooling around with it.

"No, I just need to connect it to the computer, which will wipe out the old programming uploading the new information."

She sighed in relief. "Well, let's get this over with."

Dr. Moniker placed another strip on her neck. When it took affect, he made an incision, splitting her skin to expose the chip. A long thin cord was attached from the chip to the tablet on the table.

"This will just take a minute."

As he typed a few words, a buzz filled her head.

"Should I be feeling anything?" She forced herself not to turn to him.

"A tingle is normal. If we smell something, then you should worry." He laughed quietly.

"Please tell me again why I like you, doc." She made a face, feeling like an android lying there. This was the most machinery she would ever want to have embedded in her body.

"See? Nothing to it. I want you to stay here until the numbness wears off to ensure there are no complications. A nurse will come to complete your physical." He finished up with the surgery before he unstrapped her body. "The nurse will be in to see you shortly."

"Thanks, doc." Adelaide smiled, raising her heavy arm to study the comm unit. Her old one had been a large square, about two inches wide. This new one was probably almost half the size, pretty sleek.

Dr. Moniker waved goodbye, leaving her alone to drift in and out of sleep. Her body was tired from the different time zones she'd passed on her way back to Earth.

Chapter 2

Adelaide slowly woke, blinking against the brightness shining against her lids. She flung her arm across her eyes with a moan. *What the hell was that?*

"How are you feeling?" a woman's shrill voice asked.

"In pain. How do you think I would be?" Her throbbing wrist made her snarky.

There was muttering as a clatter sounded near her, but she didn't move her arm. Something slapped against her skin and a soothing calm filled her. Shifting her arm, Adelaide sighed in relief. "How long?" she asked.

"One hour," the nurse said.

"That's it?" Adelaide asked.

"Yes. I'll be back shortly to help you up and then just a quick physical."

When she was alone, the first thing Adelaide noticed was the silence in her head. Even if ALICE wasn't communicating, there had been a constant, soothing low hum. Evidence something was watching out for her and could grab her from the razor edge of an abyss if necessary. This past year, many such circumstances qualified.

* * *

Adelaide improved quickly. Escaping from the white prison and scary nurse, she headed to the mess hall. Her stomach was a mass of knots growling its displeasure. Standing in line, she perused the options for supper, deciding on some type of noodles with sauce. She grabbed the spoon, heaping it onto her plate. At the first available empty table, Adelaide sat, scarfed down her food, ignoring the glances from the other patrons. No way did she want to entertain any questions on hostiles or her role. Finishing in record time, Adelaide dumped her dishes into the automatic sanitizer, waited for the beep then headed to her temporary quarters.

She got comfortable on the little couch in the one-bedroom living quarters before pulling up the men's service records. Somehow, the holodisplay seemed to be clearer and larger than her previous one. It even had the ability to zoom, definitely an upgrade. Made the pain running along her arm almost worthwhile.

Both men were thirty years old. Bastion fought in the Raykar wars, turning into a mercenary/assassin-for-hire after. Adelaide was surprised the general wanted him back. A mercenary could have problems with loyalty. Would the enemy entice him with a larger payout? Adelaide would need to keep an eye on him. Hopefully, he wouldn't turn on his own kind for scum like the Cradesions.

Cullen's accuracy and knowledge with weapons was impressive. The military spent extensive resources training him on every imaginable instrument of destruction out there. He even used multiple alien technology. Both were potential assets to the mission. She sent off her acceptance to the general, warned Gil of their early start then pulled up the mission data.

*   *   *

Adelaide gawked at her new ship, almost afraid to touch it. Shaped like a thin, elongated egg with the nose more pointed, its dark green colour seemed to sparkle with a thousand stars. The two long wings curved slightly to the back. Adelaide stepped closer to the open cargo ramp, resembling the mouth of a large whale. Evenly spaced along the hull were the ports for two heavy pulse phasers, six light phasers, two torpedo launchers and two cannons. More weapons were on this ship than on her last one during the Raykar wars, and the Clandestine was smaller. A small black deflector dish protruded from the side of the ship, complementing the state-of-the-art shields that were installed. After all the hardware, a small empty space was left which had "Clandestine" in capital letters. In her trance, she didn't realize Gil had stopped beside her until he snorted.

"Damn it, Gil. Don't sneak up on me." She glared at him.

Grinning he asked, "You want some time alone? Maybe wipe the drool off."

Adelaide swiped her hand across her chin, expecting to find moisture. "Don't make me smack you." She stomped towards the ship, ducking under one of the curved wings.

Gil laughed behind her.

Spinning around, she asked, "Alright, Chuckles, are you ready to see the ship or not?"

"Yep."

Man of few words. Over the years flying with him, Adelaide grew to enjoy his silence. Gil only spoke when necessary, so people learned to listened. Except when he got it in his head to annoy her. At times, during long trips, Gil decided to break the monotony with pranks or by talking her ear off, which freaked Adelaide out more than the pranks. Once, he told her all about a mission he'd led against the Raykar. She had nightmares for a week from the shit he committed against the enemy.

Her combat boots clunked as she walked up the rough plank. Adelaide took a deep breath, taking in the oil-and-antiseptic smell, smiling at the images they evoked. A faint human odour reached her but nothing overpowering yet. Once the ship was running, the air should circulate through. Not many had trampled through the corridors of the ship yet. She already felt possessive, which gave her a guilty conscience, thinking of ALICE on the ZOO.

The inside walls were a smooth white, not a colour Adelaide would have picked, as it showed the blood too well. Upon stepping fully into the cargo hold, she turned slowly, taking in the space. Two large crates sat strapped along the side next to a couple of closed metal cabinets. She walked over to the crates, the attached manifest listed different types of handheld weapons as well as armour. They must expect resistance.

"This is well stocked," Gil said poking through the cabinets. Masks and other necessary tools filled all the shelves.

"With all the fire power this ship is packing, do you think it will be an issue for speed? I'm not complaining, but we may need as much speed as possible if there are hostiles."

"I think the higher ups figure our portable jump gate will even the odds."

She chewed her lip. "Yes, but doesn't the jump gate need time to recharge after each use?"

"Depends on the distance we jump. The farther we go, the longer the recharging. It should get us away from anyone."

Dropping their bags, Adelaide barely resisted the urge to do a little jig as they went farther into the belly of the beast. The stark white continued throughout the ship, besides a thin strip of substance running along the top and bottoms of the wall. They seemed to pulse with a faint glow. Tentatively she poked a section with her finger.

"Getting to know the ship, are you?" Gil laughed.

She grinned, nodding her head. "My ship. This is new." The glow brightened along her finger trail.

A seven-by-seven monitor hung on the wall, displaying a diagram of the ship.

"Let's get the inspection done. Then we can thoroughly go over this new tech."

Gil pointed to the screen. "We should go to the medical bay first."

"Why?"

"Because that's probably where you'll spend most of your time." Gil guffawed.

"Remember I'm your captain, Chuckles I'll demote your ass faster than you can blink." Adelaide pursed her lips, keeping the smile in. He wasn't wrong.

"I'm not worried." He smirked over his shoulder as he headed towards medical. "You wouldn't survive without me."

Adelaide gave up the fight, laughing down the walkway behind him, her eyes roaming over everything.

The doors glided open, revealing a small room with two cots and state-of-the-art machines. She recognized some of them from the cargo the ZOO carried. A med bot activated, turning in their direction. It slammed to an instant stop, speaking in a low, deep voice.

"How may I be of service to you, Captain?"

Adelaide examined the machine in front of her. It was an upgrade to most med bots which were more of an oval blob. This one had a human shape which surprisingly put her at ease.

"I'm inspecting the ship before liftoff."

"Let me know if I can be of assistance." The bot returned to its previous position, watching the door.

"That's a little creepy." Gil eyed the bot, Adelaide nodding in agreement. Becoming members of the Syndicate gave Earth access to a plethora of medical advancements. Earth scientists were able to engineer the med bots. It would be an asset; she'd never had medical assistance on board while a civilian. It was always a patch job until someone qualified could be reached. But the last battle she fought against the Raykar, where there had been a med bot, it did little good. Their ship blew up—not much doctoring to be done, patching or otherwise.

Adelaide walked around the twelve-by-twelve room, considering the instruments.

"Are you programmed for all known species or just the ones we have on board?" Adelaide inquired.

The bot's eyes lit up as it faced her. "I am programmed for every known living species."

Once she finished in the medical bay, Adelaide and Gil headed out to inspect the rest of the ship. She was pleasantly surprised with the space, no claustrophobic issues to deal with.

"You get some pretty swanky quarters," Gil ribbed.

"I deserve some after having to deal with you daily. I need alone time."

"I don't want to know about your alone time." Gil grinned.

"Ew. You're like a father; we're not talking about sex." She made a face, focusing on one of the four duplicate common quarters. They held three single beds and a wardrobe. "You'll be nice and cozy in here," Adelaide said.

"I don't need much room; I'm in the engineering room twenty-four/seven. When are the others coming aboard?"

Glancing at her comm she said, "Should be within the hour." She followed Gil's hurried steps to engineering. Nothing in the other personnel's service records raised any red flags.

Gil sighed the moment they entered the room, then grinned like a kid in a candy store. The ship ran on carbidihyde like the ZOO. The portable jump gate was built into the corner of the room. A black metal box contained the unit, standing as high as Gil's shoulder. Multiple clear hoses ran from the box to a grey panel in the bulkhead. Adelaide could see blue fluid running through them. Gil pulled a tool out of his back pocket kneeling in front of the box.

"Are you done checking out the ship?" Adelaide smirked.

"You go ahead. It's your job." Gil waved a distracted hand at her. The front panel of the box clattered to the floor as it dropped from his fingers Adelaide saw his grin before his head ducked inside.

Screeching, Adelaide jerked forward. "What the hell, Gil? You don't know what's in there." She reached for his arm but didn't make contact in case she made him hit something.

His muffled voice came through the opening. "It's fine. I examined the specs already. All good." His body wiggled as he pulled himself a little farther in.

Adelaide shook her head, muttering under her breath. She would never get him out of here now. Might as well finish inspecting the rest of the ship. Gil would let her know if engineering met his standards.

Beside the bridge was a common area. Multiple chairs and couches littered the space, a small replicator sat in one corner beside the automatic sanitizer. A small square mat covered the opposite corner where the crew could work out some aggression.

Stepping onto the bridge, Adelaide grinned at the shiny equipment. She sat in the comfy captain's chair. This assignment was looking up. "Computer, this is Captain Adelaide 24001; initiate interface with my comm."

A husky male voice responded. "Yes, Captain. Glad to have you aboard. It will take two minutes."

A cord shot out from the chair's arm, attaching to her wrist comm. The ship beeped, and her comm buzzed as the screen lit up, then the cord withdrew.

"Interface complete," the ship said.

"Captain, permission to come aboard?" a voice came over the comms.

"Visual," Adelaide said, a video feed showed the outside of the ship with six people standing ready. "I'll be right there."

Adelaide messaged Gil to expect company before heading to the cargo bay to meet her crew.

*   *   *

Adelaide dragged herself to the bridge—four hours wasn't nearly enough sleep. She swiped at the hair hanging across her eyes before straightening her uniform.

"Captain on the bridge," Ensign Brigg said as the three-bridge crew saluted. She hoped Gil hadn't killed the other crewmembers assigned to the engine room.

"At ease." Adelaide parked her tired body into the chair. "Pull up the map of Tikaani." They needed to determine the best landing site. She eyed her crewmembers, trying to uncover their motives. *When did she get so cynical?*

"Captain." Gil's voice came through her wrist comm.

"Yes?"

"Our last passengers are here."

Adelaide grinned at Gil's sarcasm. "Send them to the bridge." She spun her chair to face the door and waited. Might as well establish the pecking order right off the bat. She didn't know these boys from Adam.

The door slid open; two men strode onto the bridge. Both scanned the area, bodies tense. When their eyes reached Adelaide, they relaxed slightly. They stepped closer, saluting.

"Captain," they both said.

"At ease."

"I'm Bastion. Glad to be part of this mission." His voice rasped like he had swallowed glass. His plain brown hair was razored short. A tight black shirt and pants emphasised his slim yet muscled physique.

Bastion's brown eyes seemed to burrow into hers, trying to learn all her secrets. Not liking the feeling, she stood, glancing at Cullen who—unlike Bastion—was bulky with muscles.

"How many weapons did you bring?" she asked spotting the lasers strapped to his waist.

Cullen snorted, flashing a grin. "Probably not enough." He swiped the blond hair escaping from the hair tie at the nape of his neck.

"What he considers 'not enough' could level a city." Bastion leaned against the bulkhead fingering the knife on his hip.

Adelaide smirked. "All crewmembers are aboard. We'll take off in ten minutes. You sit there in case I need you." She pointed to the open seats while perching on the edge of her chair, taking the yoke in hand. "Once we leave orbit, I'll brief you in the ready room before showing you to your bunks."

Bastion sat, turning to face the screen, body at attention.

She began take off procedures, pushing multiple buttons on the display screen.

"Gil, we're ready for take off," she called.

"Ready," he replied.

Adelaide pushed forward on the yoke. Ascending through the clouds, the ship broke orbit. With her eye on the screen, she watched for the jump gate, wanting to be farther away from any planets before trying their personal jump gate. Gil would want to inspect every inch of the tech to determine any issues.

Adelaide glanced at the two newest arrivals. "In your files it states you've previously worked together. You accomplished the missions, but there were questions about compatibility."

One of the bridge crew shifted in their seat, tapping out some notes on a digital screen.

"We were assigned to the same missions," Bastion said.

Adelaide waited for the story. When no one was forthcoming she said. "You don't get along?"

"We're fine." Cullen grinned. "He just finds my personality difficult to handle. Isn't that right, comrade?"

Bastion grunted, his gaze inspecting the bridge while ignoring Cullen.

Adelaide smirked; this might be entertaining.

"The ship's fire power appeared impressive from the outside." Cullen leaned forward.

"Yes. It's state of the art. A brand-new model. We're the guinea pigs. You can talk with Gil; he'll give a tour of the engine room. It will all be in your briefing."

Nodding, the two men settled back as the ship headed to the jump gate. Silence reigned while Adelaide maneuvered the ship through the jump-gate stream. Stars zoomed past the ship in streaks of light as the ship shot across the galaxy. The pressure forced everyone back into their seats until they reached the exit.

When they shot out of the gate, Adelaide said, "Engage cloaking. Contact me immediately if anything comes up on radar."

"Yes, Captain."

"Let's go, men." She waved her hand, walking to the ready room. Once they were all seated, she pulled Tikaani up on the screen.

"This is where we're headed. The status of their space station is unknown, there's no contact from the planet. All attempts from our probes to gather information have been met with failure. We are on a reconnaissance mission only—to ensure this was a natural disaster—and report back to command. This ship is a new protype our military developed using some of the Raykar technology. The material is lighter and stronger than ours. Not only do we have cloaking, but we are also using the only portable jump gate developed."

"Holy crap!" Cullen's brows lifted, excitement shining from his eyes.

"What are they really expecting us to find?" Bastion asked, crossing his arms.

Adelaide eyed him for a moment. "The Syndicate is unsure if it is a natural disaster or unknown hostiles. We are there to ascertain the threat."

"What is the prevailing view?" Cullen asked, leaning back in his chair eyes on the planet.

"They are thinking natural. There were solar flares in the vicinity."

"So why are they sending out an elite force?" Bastion demanded.

"We don't question orders." Adelaide's lips pulled into a tight line.

"Sorry, Captain, but I'm not sure why we're needed."

"It's because of Kahoon—right, Captain?" Cullen said.

Bastion glanced at Cullen, his eyes searching.

"It's not ours to question. I've sent you information on the planet and the Clandestine. Study it. We'll be testing the portable jump gate shortly. Since Tikaani has two times the gravity as Earth, once this briefing is complete, I'll be having the ships anti gravity increase incrementally until it's close to Tikaani's. We only have three days until we reach the planet. It's not enough to climatize completely, but this will help some. We'll also start combat training under the new gravity. It may make a difference if we have to fight."

Cullen groaned, making Bastion smirk. "How many on the boarding party?"

"Four. Us as well as Gil, my engineer."

Both men frowned but didn't comment further. They would be surprised by Gil; Adelaide believed he could take both of them if necessary.

"Good. A smaller strike force is preferable. I'm going to inspect the beauties on board." Cullen rubbed his hands.

"What about your quarters?" she asked.

"That can wait." He grinned, scurrying out like a horde of Cradesions followed. Adelaide knew she wouldn't catch any glimpse of him for the rest of the trip except for the mandatory training.

"Well, Captain," Bastion drawled.

Adelaide raised one brow, waiting, but nothing came. He just sat staring in her direction. He was doing the eye thing again.

She shifted and broke the silence. "Are you ready to see your quarters?"

"I'll be fine. I can tour our new home and will eventually stumble across it. The ship isn't that big."

She nodded at his retreating back, breathing a sigh of relief. The room seemed to lighten with the absence of his presence.

Adelaide stood, stretching her arms. It was going to be a long journey. Three Earth days before they reached Tikaani's orbit. Deciding to stay in the room, she pulled up the map of Tikaani, going over the plan again. She'd found a suitable landing site, dependant on what they discovered when they reached orbit. The site was far enough from the capital city, hopefully they would arrive undetected. The shifters weren't fond of trespassers, even well-meaning ones. She next pulled up the inhabitants. The planet was comprised of mostly wolf shifters. Intel also described bear and unknown types of felines. Since the planet rejected the Accords, other species had limited access to the planet. There was a small station in orbit, but for larger freight, the ships still landed on the planet or sent shuttles.

Adelaide's stomach growled. She'd been too excited to eat earlier. After ensuring everything was programmed into the computer, she headed towards the mess hall. Stepping up to the replicator, Adelaide grabbed a plate, put it into the machine, typing in what she wanted. Minutes later, the replicated pizza landed on the plate. Situated at the bar, Adelaide poured some toph into a waiting cup. She sighed with delight as the hot liquid slid down her throat, lovely caffeine. The flavor was like a burst of nuts in her mouth. Shovelling her food interspersed with a drink, Adelaide finished in record time. Her stomach always clenched if she left the bridge for long. A ship with a crew would be different.

* * *

"Time to wake up, men." Adelaide made sure the speakers in the quarters were loud. She grinned at Gil who stood waiting beside her. "Meet in the common area in ten minutes."

Two seconds till go time, Cullen and Bastion straggled in, grimaces on their faces. She could guess what was making them pissy; she was feeling the different gravity as well on her body. Having only a day to climatize before fighting wasn't enough.

"What the hell time is it?" Bastion grumbled, swiping his hand down his face.

"What the hell time is it, CAPTAIN," Adelaide yelled.

They both straightened. "Yes sir."

"It is 0600. I want a couple of hours training every morning and afternoon. I've brought in a few practice weapons." She gestured to the corner of the mat where a pile of staffs and swords lay. "I want us to also practice with different opponents." Both sets of eyes landed quickly on Gil then slid away. Holding in her grin, Adelaide chose a staff. "Since we don't know what we will be encountering on the planet, I want us to be prepared for anything. Have either of you used a staff before?"

"Something similar," Bastion said while Cullen nodded.

"Okay, Gil and"—Adelaide considered the other two, deciding who should be knocked down a peg or two— "Bastion, you can go first." She lobbed a staff at both men, then stepped off the mats.

Cullen stepped up beside Adelaide studying her for a moment before facing the combatants.

"Remember, your bodies are going to be moving slower; you'll need to compensate."

They both nodded at each other then dropped into a loose stance. As they circled each other, their eyes narrowed in, gauging their opponent. Gil struck first; Bastion couldn't quite hold back his surprise before shutting down as Gil hammered him swiftly, knocking him back a step. Even with the change in gravity, Gil was a force to reckon with. Soon, they were matching blow for blow, but they were slowing down, sweat dripped down their bodies. Adelaide glanced over, seeing a few of the crew standing in the entrance, watching.

"Alright—time," she called, after letting them pound each other to a draw.

Breathing heavy, both men stopped, using the staffs to hold their bodies up.

"Not too bad hold man," Bastion wheezed.

Gil nodded with a grin.

Once they were off, Adelaide twisted her long hair into a knot turning towards Cullen, "How about swords?"

Cullen smirked in agreement.

She knew he had extensive training even with swords. Earth learned early in their space exploration many planets didn't believe in laser weaponry. War—or fighting—was an artform, having to do with honor. During many ground battles, force fields prevented lasers from being used, forcing the different sides to resort to hand-to-hand or less-advanced weapons.

Pressure built in her legs as she twirled the sword, analyzing Cullen's body movements. As he arced to the left, she brought up the sword, blocking his first strike. Her arm quivered, and she countered down, meeting resistance.

Cullen stumbled back slightly out of range, grimacing at her. "Damn, it's tiring to move."

"That's why we're practicing."

* * *

When the two hours were finished, all four were exhausted. Sweat stained the mats.

"I'm heading for a shower," Adelaide said, trying to keep upright in front of them. It was slow going to her quarters, as soon as the door swished closed, she collapsed on her bed.

"I'm dying." Adelaide moaned; the aches consumed her whole body. She didn't even have a hot shower to look forward to; the gel did nothing for her condition. She decided the plan would be to have a shower, nap and if she was still sore after, head to the med bay. Her stomach gurgled its displeasure, but she had no plans of leaving her room; she was willing to starve rather than appease it.

After her nap, Adelaide headed to the bridge. Time to test the portable jump gate. She only winced a few times on the way, which was better than some of her karate training she'd endured while earning her black belt.

"Gil, you ready to start?"

"Just a minute, Captain. We're finishing the configuring."

Adelaide watched the stars whiz by on the screen. The beauty always astounded her. The universe seemed infinite; her life was up here travelling the stars.

"We're ready, Captain."

Adelaide pushed the button and waited. A whirling noise came from under the console, her screen lit up and the ship jerked forward. The familiar jump-gate colours appeared: red, green and yellow.

She smiled. "Gil, how's it going down there?"

"Alright. The sensors are showing an increase in engine temperature. I don't like the vibrations and small stutters I'm feeling."

"They never mentioned those other two issues from the testing. Keep an eye on it. We should almost be through."

"Yes, Captain."

A couple more lurches and the ship arrived into normal space. Not as smooth as a large gate, but not bad. Adelaide gave a little cheer then groaned, holding her head. The others on the bridge appeared a little green under the gills as well. She scrutinized the sensors. The jump gate had worked, allowing them to reach the designated coordinates in a fraction of the time.

"Any critical problems, Gil?" she asked.

"The engines are still hot."

"We knew that was an issue. Investigate what could be the cause. If we're running, we don't want a system failure. Send your report so I can inform the general."

"Agreed. I'll get right on it."

After activating the cloaking device so no one could see their destination, she sent her report to the general.

One more jump gate and another thirty hours they arrived. Their ship was thrown into the orbit around Tikaani.

A debris field floated close to the planet.

"Bastion, Cullen and Gil, up to the bridge now," Adelaide yelled. She could feel the vibration of the three sets of feet running down the corridor. When the door slid open, the three musketeers skidded in. The scene unfolded on the screen in front.

"Holy shit!" Cullen swore under his breath.

"Damn it!" Adelaide jerked to the left, causing the others to tilt as she avoided the bulk of oncoming objects.

The ships sensor blared a warning: "Captain, multiple objects are on a collision course with the ship."

"No shit, Sherlock," Adelaide muttered as some pieces collided with the hull. "Computer, beam in a sample from the debris into the cargo bay, erect a force field around it."

The ship hummed quietly. "Captain, it is done."

Once they were far enough away from the debris field, Adelaide said, "Let's go," waving at the three men to follow.

On the cargo floor was what appeared to be a piece of metal the size of a car door. Adelaide grabbed a scanner from the cabinet and approached the object, waving the tool back and forth.

"What is it?" Gil asked.

"The object is composed of material commonly used in space stations with a small amount of unknown organic substance." Adelaide frowned down at the scanner. "Computer, scan the planet orbit for a space station."

"There is no space station in the vicinity."

"Scan the debris field for all materials." Adelaide closed her eyes briefly, saying a silent prayer.

"Scan complete. The debris is comprised of 20.232 percent organic material. The rest consists of—" Adelaide listened with half of an ear as her heart stuttered.

It sounded like any other station material. But the percentage of living material didn't seem consistent. Hopefully, that implied survivors existed somewhere.

The station's crew compliment would've been about two thousand individuals, plus visitors.

"We'll wait for the general's response to the report and the status of the mission." After sending the report she stomped to her quarters. Scrubbing her hair under the shower gel, she let it clean away the filth from the day. She hoped they discovered the cause of the missing space station was a natural disaster because who would destroy a station with all those people?

After dressing, she prowled around the ship, eventually landing in engineering. She sidestepped as an ensign passed through the doorway. Another officer was at the control panel, frowning as he punched at the screen. Not used to the people, she searched for Gil, finding him at the jump gate.

"Gil, what's the news?"

Gil dropped his tool, turning from the console. When a grin crossed his face, relief surged through her body. Doubt hadn't entered her mind, but the quick timeframe was a surprise.

"We added frensene. Now when it's running, the heat remains constant—or even drops a few degrees. I was worried about the stuttering and vibrations, but we figured out the problem. Hopefully it will hold. Come check this out." Gil shoved his head into the box, motioning her to follow. Lowering herself to the ground, she examined inside.

"See all these tubes? Some of them were too long, making it difficult for the fluid to flow consistently. I also replaced a few parts on this motor to make it more efficient." Gil pointed his fingers to all the parts.

"Excellent. I knew you'd find the solution." Adelaide resisted the urge to give him a hug. A pat on the back was a poor substitute in her opinion, but she was conscious of the officer watching the exchange.

"Captain, General Williams is sending a transmission," the computer stated.

The grin slid off her face. That didn't take long.

"I'll take it on the bridge." Her boots slapped on the deck as she hurried to accept the call. It wasn't a great career move to keep the general waiting.

Sitting she pushed the button trying to slow her breathing. "General, what are your orders?"

"Captain." The general's face popped up on the screen. His brows were drawn together, his lips thinned. Worry showed in his face, something not usually seen on him. "The Syndicate is extremely concerned with your report. Has anything else developed?"

"No sir. We've continued monitoring, but nothing."

"Continue with the mission. Use extreme caution."

"We'll head down immediately under the cover of darkness. Hopefully, if any hostiles are nearby, they won't expect anyone."

"I want constant communication. The instant you find survivors or hostiles, I want to know."

"Yes sir."

The screen went blank. Adelaide frowned, drumming her fingers on the arm rest. Time for action.

Their plan was still the best with the information available. Command was not patient enough to wait for a probe to be launched.

"Bastion and Cullen to the bridge. Crew, prepare for entry and landing. Captain out."

"Are we still following the original mission?" Bastion asked, stepping onto the bridge.

"It's a go. Once the ship lands, we'll disembark. The capitol Smena is only a few leagues from where we'll be. Stop at the weapons armory before heading to the cargo bay."

"See you there, Captain," Bastion said as they left.

"Gil, are we ready?" Adelaide asked over the comms.

"Yes, Captain."

"Okay, let's do this." Adelaide grabbed the yoke, watching the screen. She slowly descended into the clouds. It changed from white, fluffy cotton candy to dark and windy. The ship jerked side to side, the yoke shivered, Adelaide swore, trying to keep the ship steady. Lights flashed, blinding her for a second. She blinked, tears filling her eyes. Damn it. Where the hell was this storm coming from? More lights flashed across the sky, followed by a loud boom, which rattled the ship.

"Computer, how close are we to the landing coordinates?"

"Distance is five miles."

"The surface is coming up fast."

Adelaide applied the reverse thrusters, hoping they didn't overshoot their destination.

When the ship broke through the clouds, a gasp escaped from between her clenched teeth; there was nothing. Buildings should've been visible from her vantage point, yet the ground seemed bare. No vegetation. How was this possible? Rocks jutted from the ground, reaching up like fingers to the storm clouds above.

Finding a safe spot, she dropped the ship with only a slight jarring. Wiping her brow, Adelaide unclenched her fists, flexing the stiff fingers. "Monitor our location, if you notice *anything* send it to my comm" She hurried from the bridge.

"Gil, meet us in the cargo bay." She stopped in her quarters, shoved two blasters into her hip holsters, the knives were slid into her boots. Glancing at the slim sword hanging with her other weapons, Adelaide paused. She had the feeling the sword was important. Tentatively, she touched the hilt. It was the only thing Dante had bought her as an adult, before the divide had opened between them. Breath stuttering, she grabbed the sword sliding the blade into its sheath along her back. She took the new jacket off the hook, pulling it on then zipping it to her neck. Time to go.

Her squad was waiting.

"Computer, how is the air quality on the planet?" Adelaide asked.

"It is mostly comprised of carbon dioxide. Breathing the air isn't recommended."

"What the hell? No breathing and our movement's constricted by gravity, yeah." Gil frowned, grabbing masks and night goggles from the locker, handing them out.

What could have caused the drastic change on Tikaani? Adelaide didn't want to meet whatever was responsible. As the door slid open, Adelaide's eyes grew large. The landscape was a desolate desert with a layer of fine black sand. When their feet collided with the earth, a cloud billowed allowing the wind to disperse the black particles while plenty coated their boots. Every step showed the brown cracked earth beneath. The goggles distorted her sight, but the different colours swirling above were still distinguishable. Light streaked while thunder sounded in the distance, but no moisture fell. Though Adelaide couldn't remove the mask, her gut said a burnt smell would permeate the area. Shudders ran up her spine. The men appeared just as freaked as she was.

The only noises came from the surrounding storm. Adelaide strained her ears, trying to determine if they were alone. The longer she walked, the more her feet warmed. The black ground smoldered. Pushing her wrist comm, she read through the data streaming down the holodisplay.

"Is anyone else feeling warmer?" she asked, glancing back. Three heads nodded.

"The temperature has risen by fifteen degrees since we left the ship."

The heat travelled from the soles of her feet up her legs, settling in her torso. Sweat formed under the snug black shirt. Adelaide shifted; she wasn't dressed for this. The tight black jacket was designed to protect against most elements. The technology within the jacket determined what was required, adjusting as needed. The scientists on the base had wowed her with its capabilities. They'd shoved her into the thing, practically giggling while she was trapped in a highly toxic room. Before Adelaide could finish the swear words escaping her mouth, the jacket had expanded to encompass her body covering any exposed skin. It had been fascinating. She'd grudgingly forgiven the assholes for pushing her into the room. The only reason it now covered her body was because of the mission.

When Adelaide stopped abruptly, cursing came from behind her.

"What the hell?" Bastion snarled, his shoulder ramming into her back.

"We're here." She spoke quietly. Little had changed in the landscape. Maybe a few more black hills.

"Where?" Gil asked moving abreast with her, his gun held in front.

"Smena." Adelaide shook her head at the map on the holodisplay.

"This isn't good," Gil said, slowly turning around before glancing her way. Fear shadowed his eyes, something she'd never seen before.

Adelaide pulled a vial out of her pocket, bent down, scooping up the black material. "Gil, analyze this material. I have a bad feeling about the results. Let's head back to the ship. We'll fly to the next city. Hopefully, we find answers there."

The trek back seemed to take twice as long. Everyone's shoulders drooped, and Adelaide's legs felt heavy by the time she entered the ship. Even with the few days of experience, the gravity was kicking her butt. Adelaide glared down in disgust at the black coating all of them.

"We'll leave in ten; I'm getting rid of this filth first." Making a face, she dropped her gear in the case, then headed to her quarters.

With her hands pressed on the counter, she ogled her reflection in the mirror. The black had covered most of the freckles spattered on her face. It mixed with her red hair, turning the colour to a pleasing dark burgundy. *Time to see how well the gel eats this stuff.* She peeled off the jacket, doing a double-take. No trace of the black crap remained on it. Not even shaking made anything fall to the floor. When she ran her hand along the back, it came away clean. She grinned; no way was she handing this back to the scientists. After dropping her clothes into the cleaner, she stepped into the shower.

*   *   *

Adelaide was grumpy, cursing as she left her quarters. She'd had to use the gel twice. The first spray made a lovely black sludge, dripping down her body and in her hair. Knowing her luck, the guys would be on the bridge waiting. Yup, she frowned at the two men. Gil must be down in his domain. No black was present on them. How the hell did they get clean so quick?

Settling into her seat, she pulled up the holodisplay on her arm control, flipping through the displayed map. Pushing her finger on the map Adelaide said, "This is the next location. We'll travel low and quick. The computer is analyzing all the data we collected. Hopefully the reports on the black substance will be fast."

"What do you suspect it is?" Cullen asked pacing in front.

"I don't want to voice my fears. Hopefully I'm wrong." Shaking her head, a frown marring her face, Adelaide grabbed the yoke.

"Gil, we're leaving," she announced before shooting forward. Travelling this way was better than walking. She was born to fly. It never felt right when her feet were touching solid ground. The instant decks were underneath, her stomach settled, a smile wasn't far behind. It must be from her father. Once Earth began space travel and he opened the cargo business with his friends, she flew with him at every opportunity.

The ship slowed to a hover over the city's location. Dread filled Adelaide, the same thing, nothing left. The devastation was complete.

"Computer, have you detected any ships orbiting the planet?" she asked.

"No."

"Still no life signs on the planet?"

"No changes have occurred. The results of the black sand analysis are complete."

"Put it on the screen."

The components flashed in front of them. The men swore, both sitting on the edge of their seats.

Adelaide sighed. "Just what I suspected. I'm not sure if we'll find any survivors."

"What could devastate a whole planet like this?" Bastion demanded. "There's got to be some survivors." He clenched his fists. "Computer, are there any known caves or caverns on this planet?"

"This planet had some small caves in their mountain region," the computer responded.

"If anyone escaped, that's where they went." Bastion glared at the foreign DNA, third down on the list.

Chapter 3

After informing everyone they would wait until morning before proceeding to the caves, Adelaide flew the ship into orbit, taking shelter close to the sun, where she engaged the cloaking device. She needed rest before traipsing through a bunch of caves. Her heart ached for the inhabitants as she tried to settle for the night. She hoped to God some were able to find safety.

When the next day dawned, Adelaide gave up on her restless sleep. Flipping over, she glared at the time blinking over the desk. She slowly sat up, rubbing a hand down her face. Adelaide wasn't looking forward to the search they were about to conduct. There was no way most of a planet would be hidden in those caves, not with those numbers from the analysis.

Nodding at the few crew men already eating, Adelaide grabbed her toph, taking a bit out of the breakfast bar she snagged as she headed towards the bridge. She was almost there when Gil stepped out in front of her.

"What the hell!" She stopped short, slamming her hand against her chest.

Gil grinned as she scowled at her crumpled bar stuck to her shirt. "Not so observant in your old age."

"So not funny. I was hungry. What do you want?" she grumbled, pursing her lips as he followed her onto the bridge. She dropped the rest of the bar into the garbage sitting down with a grunt.

"Couldn't sleep?" Gil asked sitting in front, spinning the chair to face her.

"Not really. Do you think we'll find anyone?"

Gil considered her for a moment. "It's not looking good. Anything else from the general?"

"No."

Gil nodded.

The door slid open, allowing Bastion and Cullen to step in. They appeared as haggard as she felt, with dark circles shadowing their eyes. Cullen's shoulder-length blonde hair stuck up around his head. Adelaide smirked, holding in the laugh. Gil, having no such compunction, let out a loud cackle, bending over his knees. Two ensigns grinned.

"Watch it old man. I know where you sleep." Cullen's lips twitched.

"Well, the gang's all here," Adelaide said. "Since everyone's ready early, we might as well head out." She twisted her hair back, tying it with an elastic from around her wrist. She kept ties hidden around her workspace and in her quarters, as allowing her wild hair to go unchecked wasn't advisable. Whenever Adelaide was tempted to chop it all off, she'd remember her afro.

The sight wasn't pretty on her thin, white, freckled face. It would look like she'd stuck her finger in an electrical circuit. She spun her chair around, holding out a tie to Cullen.

He glared at her for a moment before snatching it out of her hands. "Bastards."

"Why don't you guys gather everything we're going to need, while I fly us there. Gil, stop at the medical bay for the kit—prepare for the worst." The men left, leaving her blessedly in silence. The other crew didn't speak often, so no worries there.

Adelaide pulled up the cave coordinates. The location was on the opposite side of the planet from their search yesterday. Keeping the cloaking engaged she maneuvered to the designated entry point. As the ship descended through the dark, thick clouds, the computer beeped, announcing the cloaking system disengaged. Adelaide flew as close to the surface as possible. Hopefully if any hostiles monitored the planet, their ship wouldn't register. It was too bad cloaking didn't work on the surface. Scientists said it had to do with something in the atmosphere affecting the field which surrounded the ship.

Streaking over the black-covered ground, Adelaide fought the depression threatening to overwhelm her; she needed to stay positive. Even during the wars, she'd never seen devastation to this extent.

"We'll arrive at our destination in a few moments. The ship will stay on full alert while we're on the surface," Adelaide announced, slowing the ship. She settled gently to the ground.

"Ensign, scan below ground for life signs," she commanded.

"There is nothing, Captain."

"How deep did the scans penetrate?"

"One thousand kilometres."

Adelaide sighed in disappointment. "Keep monitoring the planet and orbit. If there are any anomalies contact me immediately."

"Yes, Captain," the crew replied.

Once she had everything required for her foray outside, Adelaide arrived at the cargo bay.

"We scanned the surface but found no life signs. Are we ready?" she asked her three comrades.

"The scanners may be blocked by rocks or metals." Bastion shrugged.

"Computer, how is the air quality?" she asked.

"The air falls within the acceptable parameters."

Cullen smiled. "At least we don't have to wear the suffocating masks."

Adelaide took a deep breath, pushed buttons on the bulkhead before walking to the opening door. Outside was as depressing as yesterday. But she could actually see real mountains made of rock, not just black ash.

"We'll split into teams. Gil, you're with me. Bastion and Cullen, head east. Keep in constant contact. The cave sites have been transferred to your comms. Even if we haven't spotted any hostiles, they could still be out there. If any survivors exist, they may react the instant we're spotted. Only kill as a last resort." Adelaide moved her hands around assuring the weapons were attached properly and none were missing from her person.

"And if we encounter hostiles?" Cullen asked.

"As long as one is left alive, shoot to kill."

A gleam entered Bastion's eyes as Cullen gave an evil chuckle, stroking the large laser gun in his hands. Adelaide almost felt sorry for anyone encountering those two. There was no square inch of empty space on Cullen's body not covered by a weapon. He was his own personal artillery.

"I want to see all the scans when we return to the ship. Computer, lock down. Don't allow any entry except to us four. If there are other bio scans, remain closed until proper authorization."

The men showed surprise.

She shrugged. "If we're being led at gun point, I don't want the enemy to gain access. Okay, let's go." Adelaide turned and walked down the platform, heading north with Gil right behind.

A breeze blew across the land, stirring up the black ash. Adelaide held back the nausea, gazing into the dark clouds. The heat wasn't nearly as high, light peeked through the swirling clouds. It was the same bleak landscape, the faint light from the sun didn't help. The clouds weren't as ominous as they had been yesterday but they held the suns rays back quite well.

Adelaide glared at the approaching mountains. What secrets were they holding? Was a community living below? She hoped to hell there was. Adelaide paused, stretching her back.

"You alright?" Gil asked.

"Yes. Just a spasm. This weight is exhausting." How did Gil still appear so spry? There were still no signs of life, the silence creeped her out. Even little bugs made noise.

Shivering, Adelaide glanced around once more then continued forward. When they reached the first rock formation, they slowed, leveling their weapons. Checking the coordinates, Adelaide turned slightly, Gil stayed a few paces behind. She tensed, waiting for a surprise attack.

"The cave is ahead," Adelaide whispered, dropping to a crouch.

Keeping still, they monitored the entrance. The scanners showed no sign of life.

"Let's go." After Adelaide put on her goggles, she scooted to the opening, peering in.

Nothing moved. Cautiously, they entered, swinging their upper bodies side to side. A dripping noise came from the back of the cave. As she stepped silently towards the sound, she switched weapons to her sword. The less lasers the better. No point in bringing the ceiling down on them. Turning the corner, Adelaide spotted a trickle of liquid seeping through the cave walls, dropping to the floor. More drops fell from the ceiling. Moving closer, she sniffed What the hell was that?

"What do you think?" she whispered.

Gil moved beside her, lowering his wrist comm below the drip, pulling away once the liquid hit. Though the comms were made from a metal found on the planet Iridia, supposedly indestructible, Adelaide wasn't sure if she would have tried the same thing. She shuffled her feet, waiting for the results.

"It's acidic water, contaminated from the limestone and dolomite in the rock. There's also an unknown substance," Gil said. Adelaide glanced up at the brown stalactites hanging just a few feet above their heads, dripping the smelly water.

They continued through the only tunnel. Straining to hear any noise, Adelaide pushed the dial on her goggles. No way was any creepy-crawly getting the jump on her. This was an alien planet—who knew what lived here? She didn't completely agree with the sensors. The bastards always seemed to survive a catastrophe. They just probably buried deep into the earth. It was the fault of her father's crew and being kidnapped by a crazy alien that started her paranoia. Before, she'd just had a healthy fear.

When they were on the planet Zartuth, the crew had a great initiation where they didn't tell the unsuspecting victim about the blood-sucking insect/bird creatures. Not funny at all. Then, when Taurian decided they should marry he dragged her to his planet Raau, she was almost eaten by a pretty flower in the jungle while escaping. No wonder bugs and plant life gave her the heebie-jeebies.

They came to a halt at a dead end.

"Nothing," Adelaide stated, taking in their surroundings. With her gloved hands on the rock face, she moved along, hoping to find an anomaly. "This is a bust." She frowned. "Let's go check out the other site." She spoke into her comm: "Alpha 3, Alpha 4, have you found anything?"

A garbled noise came over the comm a crackle and pop, then nothing.

"What could be causing the interference?" Gil asked, his weapon raised.

"Maybe the unknown material the computer analyzed." Adelaide searched the ground, grabbed a rock, dropping it into her bag. Once out of the cave, she tried again. The initial silence broke when Cullen's voice punched through.

"Alpha 1. Nothing at the first cave. We're going to the next."

"Same here. Did you just vacate the cave? We couldn't reach you."

"Yeah." Cullen sounded surprised. "We didn't try to communicate while we were in."

"We need to set a time. If we don't hear from each other in one hour go to their last known coordinates. We'll rendezvous at the ship."

"Sounds good."

Adelaide closed the display, pulling a face at Gil. "Let's get this over with." She led them to the next location on the holodisplay, stewing over the disruption in communication. If danger arose, they could be screwed. Glancing up, she watched the light show shooting across the clouds. Black ash and dirt still swirled around their feet. Little pebbles occasionally hit her legs. She felt the pokes through her pants, but the fancy jacket protected her upper body.

Adelaide pressed her comm. "Alpha 1 to ship, has anything tripped the sensors?"

"No, Alpha 1. There have been no changes."

"Stay alert. Alpha 1 out."

*　*　*

The second location produced the same results. As they stepped out of the cave, Adelaide's wrist comm buzzed. A holodisplay popped up with Cullen's strained face.

"What's wrong?" she demanded.

"You guys need to get here quick."

"What's happened?"

"May have found something."

Gil followed Adelaide as they hoofed it. They had to pace themselves or they'd arrive exhausted and be worthless in a fight.

Adelaide followed the men's dot on the display. Turning the corner around a jumble of rocks, she spotted their prone bodies on the ground, weapons trained forward.

"What do you have?" she whispered.

Bastion twisted his neck. "Something happened out there. Take a look." He scooted his body over, making room.

Adelaide dropped down, army crawling into place. She adjusted the goggles, trying to discern any movement.

"What's that smell?" She wrinkled her nose.

"We snuck over there; blood's caked on the rocks with footprints around the opening into the cave."

"Any noises or movement?" Gil questioned.

"No," Cullen answered.

All four converged on the mouth of the cave. Adelaide stopped, bending down to inspect the prints and congealed blood. She sniffed, face contorting when the metallic odour hit her nose. Glancing towards the dark opening, she tensed, expecting an attack. Nothing happened. Her body relaxed slightly, and she beckoned the others forward.

Entering slowly, Adelaide scanned the dark space, adjusting her goggles. The damp seeped into her body. Her jacket shifted, spreading warmth where it touched. She tried not to jump in surprise. Startling the gun happy nut beside her wouldn't be a great plan.

A couple of tunnels branched off in opposite directions.

"Let's split up, meeting back here." She touched her comm. The holodisplay popped out. "I want to test this cave first. Computer anything to report?"

Static filled the air, but a faint voice responded. "Nothing, Alpha 1."

"We are advancing into an unknown cave. Monitor our location, inform me if there is any activity."

"Yes, Alpha 1."

"Once we separate, let's see if these stupid things still work." She frowned, shaking her wrist.

They nodded before moving towards their designated tunnel. Adelaide watched the men's backs recede before following Gil. With a huff of irritation, she peered at the brown mush beneath her boot.

"What the hell is this?" she muttered, shaking her foot.

Gil snorted, a grin spreading across his face.

"Why don't you have any on you?" she demanded.

"Because I watch where I walk." He turned, continuing down the dark tunnel.

Swearing under her breath, she kept from smiling. *Smart Ass*, she thought.

She tapped her com. "Alpha 3. You alive?"

"Yes." His voice came through clearer; she sighed in relief.

"Okay. We'll talk later. Be careful; don't engage unless necessary."

"Of course." As the display dimmed, its light highlighted the green moss hanging from the ceiling. She was going to have to sanitize everything. Who knew what contaminates were here? Adelaide wasn't a germaphobe, but she'd heard the horror stories of explorers on new planets where the native plant life caused excruciating side effects. As the ground slope changed, they seemed to descend farther into the earth. Adelaide's body heat decreased; the jacket shifted again, and a chill drifted across her body. She grinned. No way in hell would she willingly give up this gem.

Gil stopped short with Adelaide almost running into his back.

"Did you hear that?" he whispered.

"No. What was it?"

"Not sure." They proceeded slowly, weapons raised.

A faint glow illuminated the passage ahead, casting purple shadows, which danced across the walls. Adelaide paused straining to hear. Tapping her wrist comm she frowned at the response.

"Still showing no life signs," she whispered.

Gil glanced back in surprise. "It may be mechanical?" He lifted one shoulder, turning back towards the light.

"Let's wait for backup." She motioned Gil to follow.

She continued around a few turns then stopped. "Alpha 4, are you there?" she asked into her comm.

The comm buzzed, then went silent before Bastion's face appeared.

"You have something?"

"Yes. Scans are showing no life signs, but something's here."

"We haven't discovered anything. We'll meet you." The screen went blank.

Adelaide inspected the ground before lowering herself and pulling out protein bars from her pocket. She handed one to Gil, opening the other for herself.

"Man, am I starving." Adelaide ate down the meager food with resignation. She'd never liked military rations, but someone could survive on them for days. Too bad they tasted like dirt. She knew this because, yes, her brother tried to make her eat dirt when they were younger.

A slight shuffle sounded down the tunnel. They both jumped to their feet, weapons drawn. Adelaide's stance loosened as two figures came into focus. Cullen and Bastion.

"What do you have?" Bastion asked.

"Haven't seen any movement or heard anything," Gil answered glancing down the tunnel.

"Let's get this over with," Cullen said. They all prepared the weapons littering their bodies.

"Computer." Adelaide's comm crackled, then fell silent. "Computer?" she snarled. "Damn it. We're on our own right now. Keep together. We're not sure what's around the bend." She stalked towards the light. She smirked—hopefully it wasn't figurative.

A main drawback of command was sending soldiers to die. The plan was not today. She held out a hand, halting before the flickering light touched her boots. Small, jagged amethyst crystals jutted from the walls. No way was she getting too close; they appeared deadly.

When she detected no sound, she took a tentative step forward, her eyes shifting from the rocky floor to straight ahead. Weapons at the ready, the men followed silently behind. Adelaide covered her nose with her arm, trying not to gag. A rancid smell grew the farther they walked, and she was tempted to stop. As they drew nearer to a light embedded into the cave wall, a clink reached her ears.

"Did you hear that?" she demanded looking back. More sounds filtered through the walls.

"Something or someone is down here." Gil swiped across his head when something dropped from above.

They all tilted their heads. Adelaide's lips twisted as she held in the growl. What seemed like bloody flesh clung to the rocks.

"What the hell?" Bastion growled, stepping back while Gil wiped at the dark red goo on his pants.

Adelaide studied her comm. "There is a very faint trace of DNA. Why didn't the computer pick it up before?" she growled.

"There must be a strong dampener down here," Cullen answered. "Explains why we can't communicate with the ship or get accurate life readings. The connection is intermittent."

"I was hoping survivors were holed up here. But with this, I'm not sure." Adelaide pointed to the ceiling. A shiver ran up her spine. Something terrible was down here.

Passing the light, they entered a small chamber, where an altar stood in the middle, dried blood coated the sides and top. Something may be blocking the sound, but not the stench. Adelaide choked; positive her nose hairs were burnt. More crystals grew out of the walls, with blood and chunks of flesh dripping from their tips. Her mouth opened and closed but no sound came.

"Should we call in backup?" Cullen asked in a hushed voice, giving the walls the evil eye.

"No. The powers-that-be wanted a small task force—that's *us*. Let's get the job done." Adelaide moved forward on the balls of her feet. Only one tunnel connected to the vast cavern, leading farther into the mountain, down under the earth.

She swiped angerly at the red frizzy strands of hair dangling in front of her face. Sweat dripped down her nose leaving a damp trail against her skin. Noises echoed along the tunnel. Someone was hammering; the banging was unmistakable. She put her finger against her lips as she faced the others. Someone or -thing was down there.

Adelaide barely contained her gasp. Around the corner, emancipated beings lined the cavern walls chipping at the embedded black rock. Whipping around she whispered, "Holy crap, we found survivors." Her comm readings showed no life signs. "We must have stepped through a force field. We're not alive."

"Did you see anyone else?" Gil asked.

Adelaide peered again into the cavern, searching for any hostiles. "I don't see anyone."

They all crept out of the tunnel approaching one of the workers. A woman with brown straggly hair turned her body slightly aiming her pick at a large chunk of rock. As her eyes widened, her arms dropped.

Adelaide shook her head, whispering, "We're here to help."

Tears filled the woman's eyes.

Adelaide caught a glint around the woman's neck as her brown hair shifted. Horror filled Adelaide's body. What the hell was the collar for?

Noise spilled from the survivor's mouth, drawing the attention of the other prisoners.

Adelaide waited a moment; soon words sounded in her brain.

"Run, you can't be here!"

"We're getting you out of here." Adelaide stepped closer. The men fanned out weapons raised. Two other tunnels were on the opposite side of the cavern. Twenty people held still, staring with dead eyes. Ripped, ragged fabric barely covered their bodies. Bruises and cuts littered any bared skin. What the hell happened to these people? Adelaide focused on all the bare feet standing among the rock and gravel. Most had ten toes, but a few were missing digits. They weren't neat amputations; ragged skin surrounded the exposed bone.

"Are there more prisoners?" Cullen asked, stalking to one of the tunnels, where he peered into the darkness.

"Yes, but you need to leave. They will be back."

"You all need to follow Gil back to the ship. We'll rescue the others." Adelaide gestured for them to follow.

The woman shook her head violently, clasping the collar. "It's not possible. An alarm will sound, we'll be incapacitated."

Adelaide snarled, glaring at the walls. "Do you know how to disable it?"

"There might be something in the main cavern."

"How quick will the guards converge?" Bastion asked.

"Probably forty-four dartoids."

Adelaide calculated they had about eleven Earth minutes. "How many more survivors?" she asked, watching the other captives still chisel away. "Why are they still working?" She tilted her head in their direction.

"Why stop? We won't escape. Any action taken will be severely punished. Noise is expected." The woman's body visibly shook with some unknown terror. "Only a few hundred of us are left alive."

Adelaide gasped. Out of a whole planet? "We need to disable the dampener. Alpha 2, head back the way we came. I want to know when contact with the ship re-establishes. If it's close to our location, we can beam the survivors."

Gil nodded, running into the tunnel they came from. The captives shifted, a few more ceasing their hammering. Adelaide eyed the purple glowing walls, wondering why it held any value.

Pounding feet came from the passageway. They all swung toward the noise. The tension was palpable in the cavern, licking across Adelaide's skin. When Gil came into focus, she sighed in relief.

"They just need to make it twenty feet past the large room we came through," Gil said bending over slightly, hands on his knees.

"Do you think the collars will let you reach that distance?" Bastion asked the workers.

"Maybe." her tone meek, the woman kept her gaze on the ground.

Adelaide stepped between Bastion and the woman.

"How bad is it?" Adelaide asked.

A haunted look crossed the woman's face. "Very painful. Like a thousand needles stabbed into you. Standing isn't possible. Maybe we can crawl." She shuddered, rubbing her hands along her bony pale arms. Faint scars crisscrossed her biceps. Adelaide couldn't imagine what could cause a shifter multiple scarring. Their ability to heal was legendary. From what she had heard when they shifted to their other form most injuries healed.

"We need to get everyone in this cavern to safety. Alpha 2, do you think in eight minutes the survivors and you can get to the ship?" she demanded.

"Yes." He frowned. "I will definitely need help if they collapse."

Adelaide knew his thoughts. He didn't want to be leaving her with two unknowns. Neither did she, but it was a necessity. "I need you to take point. I trust you to find me after." Adelaide gazed into his eyes until he nodded.

"When do you expect the guards back for their regular rounds?" Adelaide asked.

More of the chisels stopped their pounding while despondent faces turned in Adelaide's direction.

"They rotate between this cavern and the main one. Right before you showed up, the guards provided motivation to work hard. Showing vids of our families. We also don't want to be singled out as troublemakers, who are used by the creatures. They implant eggs into the uncontrollable prisoners. When they hatch, the hosts become food for the young. It usually takes eighty dartoids for the guards to return," the woman warned.

Adelaide gaped at her in horror. "You've seen this?"

"They have shown vids from previous captives. There hasn't been enough incubation time for the hatching. The chosen captives' stomachs have slowly enlarged."

"Is it just females?" Bastion demanded.

"No."

A few of the captors had tears run down their emancipated cheeks.

Adelaide noticed the anger on their faces. "They don't have a choice about leaving people behind. We can't collect everyone first before leaving. Once you are to safety, we will rescue the others."

"Do you know who your captors are? How many? Where they came from?" Cullen asked.

Adelaide interrupted. "We don't have time for those kinds of questions. The guards will be back soon. What kind of weapons and armour do they have?"

The woman cocked her head. "We don't know about things like that." She waved her hand towards her fellow captives. "We are farmers and artists. Most of our warriors were killed. A few are still in captivity in the main cavern. The guards have black armour, they are using laser guns and swords."

Adelaide drew closer to the woman tentatively touching the collar. "Do you know if it will kill you? Or just injure?"

"I've seen someone hit the sensors setting the collar off. It kept shocking him. While he dragged his spasming body forward. He made it past the barrier. Did him no good because those bastards were there to recapture him. They actually stood there, watching him crawl, chittering to each other." She snarled. "After they beat him to an inch of his life, he was thrown into a cage. He said the pain was excruciating but he'd rather die fighting then live as a slave." Tears filled the woman's eyes, but she blinked them back with resolve.

"So, are you willing to endure?" Adelaide asked, glancing at the other captives. "We can help drag you across. Hopefully it won't be long." They wouldn't have time to deal with any captives resisting.

The woman scurried to the others, had a quick discussion then returned. "Yes, we'll try."

"Okay, let's get going," Adelaide said. "We'll do a quick recognisance down the tunnel before you make a run for it. Keep up the noise." Adelaide studied the walls, seeing nothing unusual. "Why isn't there any surveillance?"

"There's no way for us to escape," a gruff voice responded from the end of the line.

"Which tunnel leads to the main cavern?" Adelaide asked.

One of the captives pointed to the tunnel on the right, then resumed the chipping as Gil guarded them. Adelaide, Cullen and Bastion slunk down the new tunnel, guns drawn. Stepping silently, Adelaide strained her ears for any sounds, trying to steady her heartbeat. She stopped abruptly, throwing her hand up with a hissed warning. Clanking filtered towards them; mixed in with screams of pain. A shudder ran up her spine.

Bastion tried stepping past.

"No," she said, restraining him as he snarled. "We can't help them right now. After we get the others out."

"I'm not stopping after that." He ground his teeth but moved back.

"Let's help Alpha 2 save the ones we can."

CRADESION SPECIES

OCCUPATION: SCOURGE OF GALAXY

PLANET: SIPELGAS

PHYSICAL DESCRIPTION :
*4 and a half feet tall; four arms, two legs;
hard dark blue shell; three eyes with no
eyelids*

WEAPONS:
*Swords and lasers
Advanced technology compared to other
species*

PERSONALITY:
*They were thought to have been destroyed
during the battle between their allies and
the syndicate members
A vicious species, only concerned with
conquering planets to colonize and steal
resources. They slaughter all witnesses and
leave no survivors.*

Chapter 4

Adelaide faced Gil. "Remember, Alpha 2, get the transporters ready to beam the second lifeforms show. Calibrate them to the DNA of the Tikaani people. Don't beam any of us until they are all rescued." Adelaide could see the dismay in Gil's eyes, but he nodded.

Adelaide shuffled the captives to form a line facing their escape route. She glanced back, ensuring Cullen would follow and Bastion was in place before whispering, "Run."

It took a minute before tremors ran down the shifters' bodies, and they moved as one, with Gil in front. Adelaide and Cullen followed as the captives made it to the large cavern before one by one the bodies fell to the ground, convulsing. Gil grabbed the hands of the first captive and dragged him out the room to safety. A few were trying to crawl towards freedom.

"The alarm has probably been activated. We have to get them moving," Cullen hissed, grabbing the quivering hands of two shifters, dragging them forward.

"I'm not sure how long they can endure this before their bodies give out. Is there any help on the ship?"

"Yes," Adelaide whispered. "The med bot can immediately sedate them until the collars can be removed. We need to hasten back to Alpha 4 before he's swarmed." She held in her gags as they dragged the survivors through the remains of their people. They helped move over half the captives before signalling Gil their departure. Rushing back to Bastion they could hear shouting followed by gun fire; both drew out their laser guns, increasing their speed.

The glowing crystals enabled Adelaide to partially see as she entered the cavern. Bastion was pinned down at the far end, behind an outcrop of rocks. He peered from one side, firing at the two nightmares slowly advancing on his position. Large metal feet stepped silently on the crushed stones. A dark-blue exoskeleton covered the creatures. She gawked at the four arms protruding from the body. Large helmets covered their heads with a clear face shield in front. She wondered why a weapon wasn't wielded in every hand; just two carried weapons she'd never seen. A stream of light burst forth eradicating Bastion's shield. They all ducked as rocks flew everywhere.

Cullen took advantage of their distraction, firing his laser making a direct hit as he ran into the cavern towards a rock by the entrance. The creature took a step back when contact was made. Adelaide held in a gasp—no damage at all. She raised her laser firing a continuous beam at her target's side. Disgust filled her when its head turned 180 degrees, glaring three bright red eyes in her direction.

"Alpha 3, throw something! We have to stop them," she yelled.

"Do we want to survive?" he answered back.

"At this point it's debatable. The survivors are more important."

"Find cover, or at least get farther back."

Adelaide kept firing dodging backwards to the original tunnel. Her opponent twisted his body matching the direction of its head. She dove to the right, as far away as possible. Her body hit the ground hard, forcing out a grunt. "Do it now!" she screeched.

A small ball flew over the men's hiding spot, landing at the first creature's feet. As a shock wave shattered the exoskeleton, the creature let out a high-pitched scream. Flinching, Adelaide slapped one hand over her ear while her jacket morphed, covering her head and upper torso.

She raised the gun, hand steady, and squeezed the trigger. Her aim hit the side of its neck; the creepy ass head exploded off. She grinned as the head dropped to the ground, its body bursting apart from Bastion's gunfire. Seconds later, the other beast joined him on the ground. She slowly raised her sore body, frowning at the gore coating the back of her legs. It took a minute of patting before her head was free of debris. *Sweet, no damage.*

Bastion and Cullen popped up. A grin spread across Cullen's face.

"What the fuck? You trying to kill us?" Bastion's fists clenched, a snarl on his lips.

"Don't be melodramatic. It's something I've been working on but never had the chance to test."

"Looks like success to me." Adelaide smiled. They all gawked around the cavern at the bug guts coating every surface. She covered her nose. "My God, do they ever stink. What the hell is in them?"

They crept closer to the two heads. She jerked back with a scream. "Damn it. I saw its eyes move."

They both burst out laughing, slapping their hands.

"Shut up. It's not funny." She scowled.

"The great Captain Adelaide, afraid of a little head." Bastion's grin grew.

"If anyone finds out I will kill you. Let's get moving. There's bound to be reinforcements dispatched to find their buddies and investigate the noise."

Stepping gingerly through the muck, she headed to the tunnel which led to their goal.

"Why didn't their heads explode?" Bastion questioned as his boot connected. The head bounced forward, striking Adelaide's heel.

She snarled swirling her head back. "Fuck off. Quit fooling around."

He held up his hands in surrender. "Sorry. Didn't mean to make contact."

She couldn't help noticing the twitch in his lips. Swearing under her breath, she stomped away. The quicker they could reach the controls, the better. Their battle had to have signalled someone of the breach.

*   *   *

Gil paced in front of the screen, swearing under his breath. He should be with Adelaide. Those boys wouldn't keep her safe. He could feel the two ensigns scrutinizing him. Taking a deep breath, he turned. "Anything yet?"

"No sir," one replied.

Gil's lip curled as he spun around again. He'd learned the names of his subordinates in engineering, but the other crew he hadn't bothered with. It was a given during war to lose your comrades; no point in getting close. He was there because of his promise to Adelaide and him being back on the ship did shit-all in fulfilling it. When Adelaide was younger Gil had stepped in many times to stop her brother, Dante, from harassing her when things escalated. Their father never assisted, saying they needed to work it out between them. Gil never had children, but even he knew when things became physical, someone needed to intervene. Adelaide started training and soon surpassed her brother and their scuffles petered out.

He shuddered, remembering the screaming from the survivors he'd already brought aboard. Once they passed the barrier their collars activated, shocking their wearers. The med bot put them into stasis first then began attempting to deactivate the technology. He prayed to every god he knew that because they were transporting the other survivors the collars wouldn't trigger. With no knowledge of the number of survivors, he couldn't prepare medical.

* * *

Moving slowly single file through the new tunnel, Adelaide monitored her comm hoping for a signal. She stopped abruptly. "I hear something. Not sure if they're hostiles," she whispered.

"How far away do you estimate? Are they advancing?" Cullen asked, tilting his head.

"They don't seem to be getting closer."

Cullen checked his weapon over. "I'm ready; let's go."

With a collective nod, they approached the blinking lights in the distance. Adelaide didn't have a good feeling about this. "Ambush" seemed to be flashing in bright lights in her brain. They followed the glowing crystals until the tunnel came to a sudden end. They gazed out into the vast cavern several feet below them. Cages lined the walls and hung from the cavern ceiling beside thick rust-coloured stalactites. They were filled with multiple bodies; grunts of pain interspersed with soft crying filled the air.

Large bins filled with the purple rocks sat in the middle of the room. Even from this distance, the smell of blood and urine was strong. Adelaide breathed through her nose. Below where they stood was a small, shallow pool. Something moved through the water. A few lights on the walls cast a light-blue hue throughout the area, which accentuated the blue in the four creatures' exoskeletons as they strode from one side to the other, occasionally snapping a whip at unsuspecting captives, who cried out in anguish.

Anger filled Adelaide; these bastards had to be eliminated.

"What are these things?" Cullen whispered.

"I think they're the Cradesions. The description I've heard fits," Adelaide responded, focusing on the movements below.

Cullen's head reared up. "They were destroyed."

"No. The Syndicate believes they may be responsible for Kahoon. We found an army amassing at the edge of the galaxy and suspect it's them."

Cullen swore. "If that's true, we're in trouble. Are those kids?" Cullen pointed to the cages hanging in the middle. "What's the plan, Captain."

Her brain stuttered; she didn't see any options where they would win without casualties.

"Why haven't they sent reinforcements?" she questioned.

"Maybe they don't care. Or have nothing to worry about from us," Bastion muttered, shifting into the cave shadows.

Adelaide stood higher in order to see the far corner of the cavern. "We need to find the dampener, free the hostages and escape, without any of us dying."

"No problem," Bastion said sarcastically.

She glanced over, catching his eye twitch. "We need a way down." She studied the darkness.

"Over there." Bastion pointed to their left. The ledge sloped down, ending below a cluster of cages.

"Set to kill." Adelaide's lip curled as she adjusted the dial on her laser. "If possible, keep one of them breathing. Not sure if it was because of Cullen's weapon but their thick neck seems like a weak point. To me it was easier to see from the side where their large gaping mouth isn't protecting it." A shiver ran down her back remembering all the sharp pointy teeth they had. Adelaide slapped a hand against her mouth to hold in the giggle as a picture appeared in her head. Red Riding Hood a character from an early fairy tale on Earth said to the wolf, what big teeth you have. She must be losing it.

At a crouch, they edged along the wall. Adelaide kept a close eye on the guards as they moved around the cavern. A stone spun in front of her foot. The clank made her wince.

Bastion swore quietly. "What the hell, Alpha 3."

She froze, waiting for the fallout. When no one shouted an alarm, she breathed a sigh of relief.

"We need to get off the ledge before anymore surprises. When the Cradesions move away from the captives, we'll attack." Adelaide glanced around. "Do you have any more of those bombs?" she asked Cullen.

"A few, but we don't want to set them off too close to the captives. I'm not sure what the consequences would be."

"Alright, the first chance you get, use them since it seems to damage their armour."

As the guards made another pass, she tensed her body. The instant their backs turned all three of them leapt up, charging down the ridge, firing at the large hard-shelled bodies pushing them farther away from the captives.

Bastion snarled as their lasers did nothing other than bounce off. "Throw it, throw it!" he yelled.

Cullen lobbed the small, round ball, yelling for the free captives to dive. It impacted the ground between two of the Cradesions detonating with a loud echo reverberating through out the cavern, knocking many to the ground. Adelaide fell to her knee but kept firing at the two bodies. The exoskeleton of one broke with pieces falling to the ground, leaving vulnerable places for them to target. As the screams quieted to a dull roar, she searched for Cullen and Bastion. They were only a few feet away, rising to their feet. Dodging the return fire, they raced across the ground firing at the other two Cradesions, while the prisoners took cover. Two of the prisoners grabbed the dropped weapons engaging the enemy.

Bastion swore, Adelaide glanced back noticing the blood dripping from his arm as his steps faltered. *Damn it.*

"Do you have anymore?" Adelaide yelled.

"We're too close now." Cullen responded diving to the ground as rocks flew from his previous position. "Shit that was close."

Adelaide stepped up behind one of the Cradesions, drew her sword swinging fast. Its head rolled, *three down one to go*. Swivelling to her right Adelaide watched as the last creature fell.

"We need to find the dampener before reinforcements arrive," Cullen, said breathing hard as he analyzed the equipment in the area. A large gash ran from his hair line down to his left brow. "I think that's what we're searching for." He pointed to a sleek black console hidden behind some of the bins.

"Do you think blowing it up will work?" Bastion asked, raising his laser.

"Your guess is as good as mine. I don't understand their language." He raised his arm, and they both fired together. The explosion shot pieces of metal in every direction, throwing them to the ground.

"Do you think it worked?" Bastion croaked waving his hand to dispatch the dust floating around.

*   *   *

"Now!" the ensign cried as the computer indicated the dampener was down. Sensors came alive with life signs.

"Send them directly to the med bay. We don't know how many are coming. I'll be there if any issues arise," Gil called, hurrying off the bridge. While his face stayed neutral on the inside Gil was furious, he only cared about one life sign. Adelaide was like a daughter; her survival was paramount.

Gil moved slowly between the still bodies, trying not to cover his nose as his eyes watered. He reached the med bay just as the new bodies appeared in the room. The ship was never meant to hold this many passengers, but they weren't going to leave anyone behind. Shouting orders to the med bot, Gil grabbed the closest survivor.

* * *

A few of the kids disappeared from the cages. The surrounding prisoners gasped, moving around, making the cages swing.

"It's okay, they were beamed to my ship," Adelaide yelled, trying to be heard over the screams. "They're going to be safe. We're getting you all out of here." Cullen and Bastion along with the freed survivors grabbed the cables lowering the cages to the ground.

Alpha 1?" A garbled voice came through her comm. "There is . . . interference. I'm . . . my best."

"Hurry, Alpha 2. We've got more children here; get them to safety."

* * *

A couple more were transported to safety.

Out of the few-hundred survivors, all but a handful were in cages.

Most of the captives moved in a daze out of their cages, not uttering a word. Some began herding everyone into the corner of the cavern and helping the injured.

Adelaide raised her voice so everyone around her could hear. "We're from Earth, on behalf of the Syndicate, here to rescue you. Please stay quiet. Hopefully our ship can transport everyone before more of the enemy arrives. Do any of you know if there are more of them down here?" Adelaide asked as the men systematically opened every cage.

"We're not sure. We've never been through all the joining tunnels," a younger man answered, hobbling to them.

When all the children were gone and the first few adults disappeared, Adelaide allowed a glimmer of hope to bloom. Maybe they would be alright.

About half the adults had been extracted when loud chittering came from a tunnel to the right. Adelaide spun. Creatures swarmed the cavern, roughly twenty of them. The people with weapons surrounded the survivors, firing continuously at the enemy. An ear-piercing shriek filled the cavern, everyone fell to their knees. Adelaide writhed in pain, dropping her laser to cover her ears.

"What the hell?" she yelled, hoping it would stop. A few drops of blood fell from Cullen's ear, landing beside his bent knee into the hard-packed dirt.

As suddenly as it started, the noise stopped, bringing instant relief. Shaking her head to stop the ringing, Adelaide dragged her eyes up. She met the cold, red, beady eyes of death advancing. Glancing at her laser out of reach, Adelaide yanked the sword from her back and leapt to her feet with a wobble. She swung towards the enemy with a snarl. Missing, she was hit from behind and knocked to the ground. Another light filled the space, then darkness.

* * *

"Captain, life signs are showing in a different location from the majority," the ensign informed Gil, his fingers flying across his console.

Gil tried not to snarl at the title. "Are they human?"

"No sir. They are natives."

"Why are they separated from the rest?" Gil asked pacing in front of the screen. He collapsed into the captain's chair studying the screen. "Bring them in. We need to know why they're there. As soon as they are on board, start with the main group again." Gil pushed his weary body up and headed to see the survivors. He had promised himself after the last war with Earth no more, but here he was in the middle of something big. It was a matter of time before the shit hit the fan. Hopefully they'd all survived.

Thanking whoever was listening, the collars hadn't activated as with the first batch of survivors lying in statis, Gil couldn't stop the horror filling him as he gently pushed the survivors aside. His eyes fell to the many bare, dirty feet surrounding him, some with missing or partial digits. Determining the idea of reaching the med bot was futile, he turned in the direction of the replicator. He latched onto the first coherent adult. "We need to replicate clothing for all of you. Come with me."

Reaching his destination, Gil contemplated the refugees, who were partially clothed with torn and bloody material. It was going to be a daunting task. At a guess, over a hundred bodies were squished into the room, with others spilling into the hallway. His eyes stung, and his nose wrinkled from the pungent smell wafting through the air. He peered at the machine, building up the walls in his mind so he could complete his task.

Once under control, Gil turned to the man he'd grabbed. "Once the med bot has removed the collars, we'll get you clean."

"What if they can't be removed?" the male asked, his voice hoarse.

Gil frowned. "Since they aren't harming you, we might need to leave them until you have been retrieved by the Syndicate."

"They are harming." The male snarled. "We can't shift."

Gil kept his expression still while nodding in acknowledgement. "Yes, I see. But the other survivors we rescued are being shocked by their collars and had to be put into stasis. You are at least mobile." He turned, not waiting for a response. Pushing some buttons, he asked, "How many children do you estimate are here?'

"Mmmm, probably thirty-five."

Once the machine began its job, Gil eyed his comm. "Alpha 1 how is it going? Alpha 3, respond."

When there was nothing but static, Gil yelled, "Bridge, where is the captain?"

"We lost contact. We can't re-establish communications. Sensors indicated movement on the planet close to the caverns."

"What about in orbit?" Gil demanded running to the bridge.

"Nothing on this side of the planet, but a ship has entered the planet atmosphere on the other side."

"Damn it! Fucking bastards!" Gil skidded to a halt beside the captain's chair. "Show me."

Gil glared at the blip on the screen in front then at his wrist comm. Where in the hell was she? He didn't want to leave her. If it was just the other two, he'd be out of there in a heartbeat.

"Is the ship advancing?"

"No. It's holding position. The movement on the ground is confined to the cavern area."

"Computer what type of ship is in orbit?"

"Unknown. Fire power exceeds the Clandestine three times."

"Great! Keep monitoring. If they shift at all inform me at once."

"Yes, Captain."

"I'm not the captain," Gil muttered under his breath. But he wasn't sure if getting the real captain back was a possibility.

"Let me know the instant you reconnect with Alpha 1." Gil stomped back to the survivors.

Chapter 5

Feeling trickled back into Adelaide's body. She blinked, allowing light to filter in. A groan escaped from her lips as she shifted on a hard surface then opened her eyes wide. Bars surrounded the hard cot she lay on. The cage was dimly lit by a flickering blue light hanging outside in the corridor. Cullen's and Bastion's still forms lay on either side of her in their own accommodations.

"Hey, you guys alright?" Adelaide whispered hoarsely. How long were they unconscious? She could feel vibrations through the solid metal wall her back rested against. Adelaide pushed up, resting a moment as her vision blurred and head pounded. "*What the hell happened?*"

She propelled her body towards Cullen, legs jerky, her knees almost collapsing. Gripping the bars, she leaned forward. "Alpha 3, wake up!"

He groaned in response, rolling his body her direction but overshooting. He fell off the edge, swearing a blue streak as he hit into the hard floor.

Adelaide slapped her hands over her mouth. "You, okay?"

Struggling to rise, he muttered, "Fan-fucking-tastic. Where the hell are, we?"

She lowered her hand. "Not sure. I'm guessing a ship. They at least bandaged you up."

Cullen's hand touched his forehead running a finger lightly over the bandage. "You know how long?"

"No. I just woke. Do you have any clue what happened?"

"Just the shrieking a bloody ear, then nothing."

"Anything else wrong with you?" Adelaide asked, testing her sore limbs. Did the bastards drag her body over ever bump they could find? She was getting sick of captivity. If she were a weaker individual, she'd start believing she wasn't good anymore.

Bastion sat up on his cot using his hand for support on the mattress. Shouting in pain, he cradled his arm.

"Well, that answers the question about your injuries. I wonder why you weren't healed but Cullen was. It can't be anything good. Where is everyone else?" Adelaide stared at the empty cells across from them, the silence unsettling her. Quite a few people had still been in that cavern. Unless Gil happened to save more before she'd passed out.

Adelaide tried activating her comm. Nothing. She was grateful cutting off her hand hadn't been an option. The Cradesions' tech must be highly advanced to disrupt her comm unit.

Muted clicking and screeching reached her ears, the sounds growing louder as all three backed away from the front bars. Of course, the shadows wouldn't hide them from their captors, but maybe they would venture into the cells. Two things came into view, wielding large laser guns. One was wearing the exoskeleton without the helmet. It stood about seven feet tall while the other, without an exoskeleton, was only about four and a half feet. The short one's dark-blue body consisted of three small segments with four arms. No wonder they needed the exoskeleton, being so small another species could easily overpower them. They blended into the black hallways, raising the hairs on her arms. They stopped in front of Bastion, chittering and gesturing at him.

"What the hell do you want?" Bastion snarled, shifting slightly to hide his arm.

The tall creature, ignoring him, tapped a series of buttons on the pad he was carrying, the door swung open. Bastion rushed the enemy but skidded to a stop when the laser pulsed at his head.

Adelaide screamed as Bastion dropped a second before contact.

"Leave him alone, you bastard!" Cullen yelled.

The short one turned to them, waving the gun while the other grabbed hold of Bastion yanking him closer. Bastion's resistance didn't last long as his damaged arm was twisted behind his body. His face turned white as he stumbled into his captor. There was nothing either Adelaide or Cullen could do as Bastion disappeared through a doorway at the end of the dark corridor.

*   *   *

Watching the survivors stumble by, their shoulders drooping, the collars glittering under the pale light in the hallways, Gil dreaded the call he was about to make.

"Computer, take us into orbit, engage cloaking, hold steady in the debris field."

He hoped if Adelaide made contact, they could still reach them in time. Waiting on the surface was no longer a viable option, as the unknown ship had flown into the atmosphere. Gil couldn't risk the survivors; Adelaide wouldn't forgive him if they were recaptured.

"Captain, you are needed immediately in the medical bay."

Gil moved from the bridge, praying it wasn't dire news, they didn't need anymore. "What is it?" he demanded as the med bot moved toward him.

"I have concerning results on some of the survivors."

Gil glanced around, feeling hundreds of eyes staring their way. "Show me in the office." He strode to the little room and waited for the med bot to join him before shutting the door. "What is it?"

The machine glided to the computer and typed a few minutes before moving over. "These are the scan results from twenty of the survivors."

Dread filled Gil as he moved closer, reading the results. "What does this mean?"

"Fertilized eggs are in their abdomens. Data shows a one hundred percent DNA match to the Cradesion species."

Gil stared at the bot in horror, "Is it safe to have them on board?"

"At the moment, they seem to be in the early stages. I would recommend putting them in stasis, that might slow them down."

"Can't you remove them?"

"Not at this time. More study will need to be done to ensure the procedure doesn't harm the patient."

"How is keeping those things in not harming them right now!" Gil yelled.

"The eggs seem to be similar to an embryo at this stage and only growing and taking nutrients from the host body. That doesn't do any harm."

Gil paced the tiny room dragging his hand down his face as he swore a blue streak. "Fine. But in no circumstances do you tell anyone the real reason. State their collars are malfunctioning and this is for their safety. Where are we going to get twenty stasis pods? There are only a few in the cargo bay."

"I can't lie to my patients."

"Yes, you can. That is an order. We don't need mass hysteria on this tiny ship." Gil slammed the door open and stomped back to the bridge. Adelaide had better show up soon; he couldn't handle this.

*   *   *

Adelaide paced her cell, waiting for Bastion to return. He *had* to. The silence was deafening after listening to the continuous horrifying scream which had echoed from down the corridor, sending a cold shiver up Adelaide's spine. Doubt now consumed her mind. The search of their cells revealed nothing, no weaknesses or items to use as a weapon. Their weapons had been removed from their motionless bodies. Survival did not look promising. Was Bastion going to make it? What were they doing to him? They waited and brooded with the silence only filled by periodical metallic clicking. The vibrations against her back soothed Adelaide into a restless sleep.

"Something is coming." Cullen's whisper woke Adelaide.

She stood, walked to the bars, peering into the darkness. Two different Cradesions dragged Bastion by the arms. His body was slouched, his legs bouncing on the grey metal floor.

"What the fuck did you do to him?" Cullen demanded.

He was ignored as they stalked past, pushing Bastion into the waiting cell. The door slammed shut; the bugs waved their weapons at them, then disappeared. Adelaide ran to the bars, stretching her fingers through, trying to reach Bastion's curled form laying on the floor.

"Is he dead?"

"I don't think so. His chest is moving," Adelaide answered, worried, nonetheless. She focused intently.

"Alpha 4, wake up. You're not going to let these assholes beat you."

In reply, a faint gasping gurgle erupted from his mouth.

Damn it. She glared at his still form, searching for any minute movement.

Bastion coughed again, groaning as he shifted his body.

"Come on, wake up so you can tell me how superior you are too me," Cullen called.

In a whisper filled with pain, Bastion replied, "Course I am; you never would've survived."

Adelaide swung her gaze, grinning at Cullen before turning back. "We thought we lost you."

"Not bloody likely. I'd never give them the satisfaction." He spit a red blob by the bars.

"What happened?" she demanded.

"The usual torture, but they've upped the ante with their life saving skills." Rattling came from his chest as his brown eyes slowly opened. Pain filled them.

"What do you mean? They tortured you, then healed you?" Adelaide hissed, shaking her head in denial. No one could be that sadistic. Even during war interrogations, the prisoners were never really healed between questioning. She knew the other side; the Raykar tortured for information, killing the prisoner immediately after.

A distant but unmistakeable clattering sound drew near. Both Cullen and Adelaide jerked upright standing stiffly. Bastion groaned feebly, dragging his body close to the thin brown cot welded to the corner walls of the cell.

Two identical Cradesions came into view without their exoskeleton's on, their four-and-a-half-foot stature just reaching the top of the cell locks.

Adelaide held in her smirk, it was hard believing these creatures were the scourge of the galaxy, feared by everyone. She glanced over at Bastion but was willing to alter her beliefs.

The creatures did have the terrifying chompers, they gave Adelaide the creeps more than making her scared. Halting in front of her cell, they waved their four appendages in her direction. Even in the dim lighting, she could make out dark-blue swirls in the hard shells covering their small bodies. A segment ended close to the ground with two hairy legs culminating in claws.

"You humansss, we have determined the necessity of learning your primitive language." The first creature glowered at her with it's three red eyes.

"What do you want?" Adelaide demanded.

"Total annihilation and control. We will purge thisss galaxy."

"Yg ctg pqv zqst strict ugtxcpvu." (We are not your urgpar servants).

Her head shot up. A Raykar stomped his four-toed feet up the corridor, carrying a tray in their direction.

Rage filled Adelaide; she sprang to the bars, gripping them. Her fingers turned red as she yelled, "What the fuck are *you* doing here?" She shouldn't be surprised the fuckers were working together. How did the bastard know how to make those clicks? This Raykar didn't appear like the others in his race that she'd seen. His scales were a lighter green, and the spikes along the top of his head were larger. The Raykar were a brutal warrior race, mercenaries for hire.

"We rule; you follow." The little thing pointed at her cage with a claw. The Raykar shoved the tray along the floor through an opening of the bars.

"Eat," the Cradesions ordered.

Adelaide regarded the tray, then glanced over to each side. "What about them?" she demanded, wrinkling her nose at the grey sludge on the tray.

"It has been synthesized with all nutrients you need. They will receive later. You require now." The two clicked between themselves, their mouths opening to show sharp, pointy teeth.

Were they laughing? Adelaide wondered, reaching down to pick up the tray while keeping her eye on the enemies.

"Go ahead, Alpha 1. Don't worry about us," Cullen said from his perch on the cot.

Adelaide dipped her two fingers in and shoved them past her lips. It wasn't necessary to chew; the sludge slid to the back of her throat. Swallowing, Adelaide gagged as the smell reached her nose.

"My God. Couldn't you at least have made it a little appetizing? If you want to kill us, just have this as an offering."

Cullen laughed. "You don't have to share."

"You eat, or he ssshove it down for you," a Cradesion said, pointing at the Raykar.

Adelaide analyzed the Raykar, deciding if it was possible to escape. Slowly moving her hand, she consumed more of the sludge.

Her cell door was wrenched open, and the Raykar marched in. He grabbed her arm. "Let us go. The fun will begin shortly."

Adelaide was amazed the Raykar could form the words so well without any real lips.

His small, rounded snout pulled back in a snarl.

Adelaide twisted her body, bringing her clenched fists down on his neck, making his body drop slightly to the right height for her hands.

"You can't take her," Cullen yelled, standing at the bars glaring at their captors.

"Do not worry, your turn will come," the Cradesion said, aiming his weapon in Cullen's direction though still focused on Adelaide.

Following the direction of the gun, Adelaide froze. Her shoulders slumped as she loosened her hands around the Raykar's neck. She was marched down the corridor and into another room. Adelaide squinted, trying to make out the objects around them.

"Rav jlt vjiti."

The Raykar pushed Adelaide to a large table. Spotting the dried blood, she struggled against the hold on her body. Her crew weren't being threatened now. The Raykar wrenched her up, slamming her on top of the table, knocking her head. It was a minute before she could move but her legs were already clamped to its surface.

"Fucking assholes, let me go!" Adelaide's fist connected with the Raykar's jaw. Satisfaction surged as his head snapped back and he hissed out angerly. His cold, tiny black eyes glared at her before he grabbed her wrist, snapping the cuffs around it. Adelaide's body now immobilized, she eyed the Cradesions, tracking their movements.

"What do you hope to accomplish? The Syndicate won't back down."

"They will not ssssurvive. In the end, everyone will bow down."

"That worked well for you last time, hey?" Adelaide sneered as one of the Cradesions stepped closer, holding a large pointy instrument. She still couldn't tell the difference between the two. There didn't seem to be any distinguishing features. Did they have different sexes? Were they both males? Their coloration differed from each other. Blue swirls covered the one, while the other had stripes with less color.

The creature clicked loudly, waving one of its arms before saying, "Was a mistake. Will not happen again." It then stabbed her leg, tearing a scream from her. Holy crap, what was that thing?

"We will sssee how brave you are once we finish," the other Cradesion said from across the room. When the Raykar laughed, Adelaide vowed he would be destroyed. She gritted her teeth as the tool was impaled deeper in her leg.

"Sssscream all you want. We like the noise. Tells us we are doing this correctly."

"I won't give you the satisfaction again, you bastards."

"They all do in the end."

Adelaide observed the blood squirting and pooling on the table. How long would she last?

"Niw av vii kuy vki tiefwv wu enpuvw eprawewouq."

The other bastard brought over a larger spinning tool, Adelaide flinched, rattling her cuffs.

"This won't hurt much." The Raykar moved closer, his eyes following the tool's trajectory to her arm.

"What the hell are you doing?" She tried to keep her voice level but didn't believe it worked. The spinning tool bit into her arm, there wasn't any holding back the scream erupting from her throat. Before passing out, Adelaide saw the other Cradesion marking on the pad it held.

* * *

Adelaide's eyes flew open, the stabbing of a needle waking her. The Raykar was gone, but there were now three Cradesion torturers.

"Did better than the other."

Even though her body was fatigued, she could feel her arm. Peering down, Adelaide couldn't believe what she saw. It was whole. Blood coated the table and her body, but everything was intact.

"What do you want?" she rasped.

"To understand," one answered, stabbing her body repeatedly.

Adelaide felt each bite of the knife entering and exiting her body. Bile filled her throat, she spewed onto the floor, hoping one of the creatures was covered. Adelaide couldn't count the number of times she passed out or saw the light before being revived. The creatures didn't question her once, nothing about Earth's military, or their plans or mission objectives. Just hours-long body study. After every healing, Adelaide took longer to recuperate. Her body was fatigued, dragging her eye lids closed until something sharp entered her body.

Finally, the tools were set aside, and one of the Cradesions clicked into his pad while hopping down from the stool.

Little runt. If Adelaide could move, she'd punt him across the room.

Another Raykar entered the room, his two blasters in straps on across his chest. They didn't need a lot of armour, as their scales protected them. He stepped by her head releasing the arm straps, then held her down. The Cradesion in the room released her legs.

"You are done. We will decide on you later. Time to recuperate." The evil little thing laughed, waving its claw for the Raykar to manhandle Adelaide off the table. He was the only thing holding her up though not very well as Adelaide's legs collapsed. She swore as her body almost met the floor. Her condition was their fault; they'd have to help move her towards her cell.

Grunting under Adelaide's weight, the Raykar dragged her down the corridor. She grinned in perverse pleasure even though the sharp metal on the corridor floor occasionally cut her legs and bare feet. The brown top the enemy had put on her just reached her knees. When she stumbled, cool air blew beneath the shirt. Why in the hell did they give Bastion pants as well? A shiver of apprehension ran through her as she glanced at her guard. She had heard about the Raykar during the war and what they did to human women they captured.

Both Cullen and Bastion, who seemed much better, stood by the front of their cells. Seeing the pity in their faces, she snarled. Adelaide survived—she was strong. No pity required. Letting her body lie where it was thrown was a given. Even if she'd been healed there was no strength to be found.

"Alpha 1, are you alive?" Cullen asked. "You were gone a long time."

Adelaide flopped her limbs so she could see Cullen. "I'm terrific. Just give me a moment to move. I already have a plan for what I'm doing to all the parties involved."

Cullen grinned while Bastion gave a chuckle.

"Did you also figure a way out while on your vacation?" Bastion asked.

Adelaide managed to hold her middle finger towards Bastion. Then, after putting her hands beneath her body, Adelaide pushed. Groaning, she stumbled to the bed collapsing. "Did anything happen here while I was in surgery?" she asked.

"No one came. I'm surprised we weren't questioned," Cullen answered. "Did they ask you anything?"

"Nothing. I don't understand what they want. Have you discovered an escape route?"

"No. There's no way out of the cages except through the doors. We'll have to overpower them when they open."

"No problem," Bastion retorted.

"No weapons and soft puncturable skin. That'll work out well," Cullen muttered.

"Quit whining. We'll have to time it. I'm guessing you'll be next."

"I'll be ready." He cracked his knuckles pacing around his space.

"I'm going to pass out now. We need our strength." Adelaide closed her eyes with a sigh. It wasn't long before her breathing evened out.

Chapter 6

Gil slammed his fist on the chair's arm, making the ensign sitting in front jump. Time was up; he couldn't wait any longer. They were lucky one of the unknown vessels hadn't discovered their location yet.

"Computer, put a call into General Williams."

The comms buzzed before the general's face appeared on the screen.

"Where is Captain Adelaide?" The general pursed his lips as his brows shifted.

"I can't re-establish a connection with the team."

"What is the status of the mission?"

"I have one hundred fifty survivors on board who need medical attention. I am sending you a report. It also contains an issue with some of the survivors."

The general's shoulders fell slightly "I will send you the rendezvous coordinates."

"What about the captain. Sir?" Gil forced himself to tack on the final word.

"I will inform you of our decision." The screen went blank.

Gil swore, his body stiff as he glared at the empty screen. He'd been in the military long enough to know what the response would be, and Gil wasn't going to accept that answer.

"Once we receive the coordinates, fly us out of the debris field and engage the jump gate." He pushed from his seat and stomped to his cabin. Scratch that— to Adelaide's. He'd moved his things over a few hours ago, giving up his space to the survivors. Time to come up with a plan B.

*   *   *

Gil glared at his comm as the signal rang. "What?" he bellowed, not in the mood. The general's response arrived a few minutes before. What the hell was Earth thinking? They wanted to allow the eggs to develop to full term so they could study the creatures. After this mission, he was done with this shit. Earth was no longer on his approved associates list. There was no way he would hand over those twenty survivors without a fight. He might as well go down in a blaze of glory, not just AWOL and stealing a military ship but taking away their potential captives. Gil didn't care if this was war; they weren't going to stoop to the enemy's tactics. He needed to act now before time was up.

Walking onto the bridge Gil ordered, "Ensign, enter these coordinates." He rattled them off as he sat down.

The crew looked at him in surprise, "What about the rendezvous?"

Gil glared around the bridge. "I am the captain. We need to pick up supplies before we continue."

"Yes sir."

"How long?" Gil demanded. He had picked a planet on their route so as to not delay enough to cause suspicion.

"Approximately an hour, sir."

"I want us at top speed. Contact me when we arrive. No other communications are to leave this ship."

The crew stared at him in shock and suspicion.

"I don't have to justify my orders to you." Gil almost snarled. "You follow orders. Understood?"

"Yes sir!" they all responded as he stormed off the bridge.

*   *   *

"We're coming up to the coordinates." the update sounded from the comm.

"Dock with the space station and open the cargo bay," Gil ordered, leaving his quarters.

"Hello." Gil said softly, kneeling in front of a little girl who looked around eight years old. She sat in the corridor beside his quarters.

Tears streamed down her face. Her thin, bruised arms were wrapped around long spindly legs. She looked up and whispered, "I'm all alone."

Gil's heart broke. "What about all the people here? Don't you know anyone?"

She shook her head silently.

"Come here." Gil opened his arms, and she crawled in, clutching his shirt. He carefully engulfed her quivering body, trying to control his anger. "Was your family with you in the cave?"

"My mom."

Gil held back a flinch, "Can you describe her? Where did you see her last?"

"They kept her away from me. There was something wrong."

"How do you know?"

"She was complaining about being sick and kept rubbing her stomach."

Gil swore softly. "Well, my captain is working on rescuing the other survivors."

Her large brown eyes blinked, a frown forming on her face. "Aren't you the captain?"

The question came out with a lisp, and Gil noted the missing front tooth. "I am the acting captain. She should be returning soon—and watch out then."

"Why?"

"Captain Adelaide doesn't stand for shit like this." Gil clapped a hand to his mouth as the girl giggled. Crap, he wasn't supposed to talk like that.

He searched the surrounding faces. Locking onto an older woman, he slowly stood, still holding the girl.

"Excuse me." Gil said as the woman faced him. "This child needs someone to watch over her."

"I want to stay with you." The girl grabbed harder onto his shirt.

"Oh, sweetie, he needs to run the ship and get us to safety."

"Will you?" she asked.

"Yes. We're meeting with another ship to take you away from all this." Gil regrettably handed her over. "You will be safe." He nodded at the woman before hurrying away. The little girl brought back feelings of comfort and joy, which he couldn't afford right now. Hard choices needed to be made and worrying about feelings wouldn't help. There was rarely anyone Gil spent personal time with other than Adelaide. She was the one person who Gil accepted hugs and loving restrictions from.

The cargo bay doors were just opening when he reached them, and he spotted the contact standing ready.

"You have enough?" Gil hollered walking down the ramp.

"Yes," the man said. "What do you need all these for?"

"Classified. Get them in quickly." Gil stepped aside as a loader drove past into the ship with the first batch. "I sent you payment."

"Received. Thanks for the business."

They shook hands, and the man headed to the station entrance.

Once the cargo was stacked and inspected, he slammed the button to close the doors and pressed his comm. "Ensign, get us out of here."

"Yes sir."

Gil braced himself against the wall as the ship shuddered disconnecting from the docks. After grabbing a sled, he began heading the cargo to the med bay.

Every few meters, he had to stop and wait for someone to move out of the way. There were offers of help, but he declined. The fewer people knowing the plan, the better. One by one, the infected people were placed into the pods, and the machines were activated. Hopefully the development of the infliction could be slowed down until they found a way to help. He explained multiple times that moving the pods close to engineering was to ensure they would not be damaged or in the way.

When done, he headed to his quarters. By the time he reached his room, Gil was aching to hit something or someone. Everyone wanted his attention and answers, something he didn't have. Exhaustion dragged on his body, highlighting his age, but there was no time for rest. They should be at the coordinates soon. Maybe a shower would help—and food. When was the last time he ate?

* * *

The ensigns voice came through the ship. "Captain you're required on the bridge."

Sighing, Gil rubbed his hand down his face. "I'll be right there." His place should be in engineering, not dealing with this political crap. He stood slowly, stretching his cramped body. Five names glared at him from the data pad on the table. His finger hovered over the "delete" button a moment before he pressed it and headed to the bridge—time to lighten the load.

After situating himself in the captain's chair, Gil pressed a button on the arm. "Attention, crew. We will be arriving at the rendezvous in ten Earth minutes. All crewmembers are needed to help the survivors board the arriving ships. We will then convene for a debriefing with the other ships' captains." Gil released the button and caught the two ensigns staring at him in surprise.

"Who'll pilot the ship?" one asked.

"The computer can handle it for a short time. That's what it is for, it's not like we will be travelling anywhere." Gil growled.

"Yes sir." They both turned back to their consoles. Gil didn't miss the look that passed between the two.

"Sir, a call is coming in from the Valiant," the computer droned.

"Patch it through."

"Captain of the Clandestine?" A large man filled the screen, his jowls quivering as he spoke.

"I am the acting captain. Captain Adelaide is on a mission."

"We're here to take possession of the survivors and transport them to Segundo. Prepare for docking procedures."

The Clandestine gave a shiver as the other ship attached to its access port.

"Ensign, initiate decompression; then, open the doors and come assist the transfer." Gil left to gather everyone. They would need help moving the patients in stasis, the ones with the armed collars, and now he had to ensure the pods were kept separate.

Gil glanced at all the crewman squished together by the access-port doors; something was off. Counting again, he grimaced. Someone was missing. He rushed to engineering, bursting into the room.

"Edward!" he yelled. "Get your ass out here."

A young, skinny blond man came around the corner. He shoved his hands into the oil splattered coveralls, stomping the black boots on the metal floor.

"I'm not leaving. You're going to need help."

Gil shook his head. "I don't have any idea what you're talking about."

"Don't bullshit me." Edward frowned. "I know you're up to something."

"This will ruin you."

"My choice." Edward took a few steps back.

"Fine." Gil threw his hands up in the air. "Don't tell me I didn't warn you. Since you're in, I need you to move the patients in the pods to the room behind engineering. I'll open the door. Make sure it locks when you close it." Gil sent the information to Edward's comm.

"Why are we hiding these people?"

"It's need to know. Get it done quietly and quickly. I've already segregated the ones we need. Ensure no one sees you. I'll keep everyone away."

"Yes sir," Edward said, placing his wrench on the bench and running out of engineering.

Fuck, fuck, fuck . . . Gil swore as he rushed back to the others. He needed to ensure no one noticed Edward's absence or the other stasis patients. Hopefully in all the commotion the other survivors wouldn't say anything either. This could really blow up in his face, but what other choice did he have?

* * *

Once all the survivors were settled, the crew headed for the debriefing. With everyone off the Clandestine, it was easy for Gil to convince anyone who asked that he was dealing with the pods, while they needed to be concerned about the other survivors. The new crew didn't know how many bodies were in stasis, and he didn't encourage them to question where the baby makers were. The idea still made him sick to his stomach, and the sooner Gil could disappear with the ship, the better. He tallied up the bodies filling the room until he was sure everyone was accounted for before booting it back to the Clandestine.

As he sealed the doors behind him, he yelled, "Computer, disengage from the Valiant. Edward, get ready to punch it!" Gil ran to the bridge, loading the first coordinates. With a hiss, the ship jolted as they pulled away. "Edward, now!" The engines revved, and Gil slammed the yoke forward, shooting away from the others.

"Incoming message," the computer announced.

"Ignore," Gil snarled as he pushed buttons, shifting the ship "Ready, set, go," he muttered, before activating the jump gate. The ship was spit out close to the orbit around Zartuth.

Gil sent their information to the station, then waited for approval to dock. It wasn't long before the acknowledgment was sent, and Gil maneuvered the ship towards their assigned bay.

"Edward, I need you up here now."

Gil felt the slight vibration as pounding came from down the corridor.

"Yes sir," Edward said, breathing heavily.

"I have to go planet-side. I need you on the bridge monitoring the station. I don't trust anyone here."

"Where are we?"

"Zartuth."

Edward's eyes widened as he groaned. "Why?"

"Backup. Contact me immediately if anyone approaches the ship. I'll return as soon as possible."

Gil stopped at the weapons cabinet, where he pulled out an assortment of knives and laser guns. Once they were all strapped to his body, he strode to the cargo ramp. There, he entered the code to lower the ramp. Shoulders tense, he took a few steps onto the space dock.

"Watch out," he snarled, jumping back as a loading pad clipped his foot.

Screeching came from behind the pad. "Virl hai!"

Gil glared as a six-foot feathered freak walked into view. He whipped out his laser. "You just keep walking."

The creature flapped his feathered arm in Gil's direction, stomping his webbed feet past the ship. Gil monitored the creature's path until it entered a ship at the end of the dock. Gil didn't have a good feeling. If these things were out and about, nothing positive ever came from it. Most civilizations considered them scavengers, like the Raykar.

"Edward, lock down the ship. I spotted a Ptica."

A smile stretched Gil's lips as he listened to Edward swear. "Keep alert."

"Will do, sir."

Time to find some reinforcements, Gil thought, heading towards the Green Sector of the station. Most tried to stay away as this location was used for the more illegal and dangerous activities. Not that the whole station wasn't one large den of iniquity.

"Stop!" a quiet, thin voice cried out on Gil's left.

He stopped, drew his weapon and waited.

"Quit fighting," a deeper voice ordered.

Gil peeked around the corner into a corridor to assess the number of assailants. A growl erupted from him. Two human men held the slim arm of a boy as they tried to put a collar on him. Gil crept closer, wrinkling his nose as a putrid smell wafted from the bodies in front of him.

"I wouldn't do that if I were you." Gil raised his weapon.

The two men spun around, keeping a firm grip on the wriggling kid.

"Leave now, and we won't kill you." The man's blackened teeth showed through his snarled lips.

"I don't think so," Gil said. "Let him go."

The two glanced at each other, giving a nod. One man slowly released his fingers from around the boy's arm, while at the same time the other raised his laser.

Gil dove to the ground, firing twice. The two bodies collapsed, and the boy took off.

"Hey, wait!" Gil yelled at the kid.

"Still the hero, hey." A gruff voice laughed behind him.

Gil stood, slowly turning around with a grin.

* * *

Adelaide's body jerked as a loud clank disrupted her nightmare. Thankful to escape the black, dark creatures chasing her, Adelaide tried opening her eyes. Gunk stuck to her lashes, making it difficult. She rubbed them in frustration, feeling the wetness on her cheeks.

From what they'd calculated their vacation had been four long tortuous days. Even though they were medically healed, their bodies weren't adjusting. Adelaide could imagine the miracles the Cradesion's tech could create if the Syndicate had control of it.

Slowly standing, she checked her balance before running on the spot. They'd all agreed exercise was essential in preparing for escape, the first opportunity available. It was also a distraction; having to listen to each other's screams was devastating. *Who was she kidding?* Nothing could block out the noises. The only consolation was Gil had hundreds of survivors— Adelaide needed to believe they'd escaped. Or it was all for nothing. Their captors implied that the remaining captives had been killed, with only her crew remaining. She prayed daily that wasn't the case, hoping there was a chance of rescue.

She winced as her feet landed on the cold metal floor, leaving spots of blood as they lifted. Focusing on the purple bruises and cuts littered across her feet, she tried moving quicker. This wouldn't stop her; they wouldn't break her. A few teardrops splattered to the floor. Angerly, she swiped at her cheeks, taking in a huge breath before dropping to the ground for a set of push-ups. As her body heated up with exertion, she grimaced as her own body odour reached her nose.

By the time she finished, Cullen and Bastion were moving in their cells. Adelaide grinned, "Hurry up, boys. You're behind." After what had happened the other day, she made sure her legs were pointed to the back of the cage, laughing at the memory of Cullen's and Bastion's faces as she flashed them, damn shirt.

"Don't worry Alpha 1, we men will have no problem catching up," Bastion commented as Cullen laughed.

Collapsing beside her cot Adelaide watched the others finishing their work out.

"Do you think we can beat them?" Cullen asked breathing heavy.

She shook her head, "I'm not sure. Look at their technology and how difficult it is to kill them."

Bastion grunted as he sat. "What about that fleet you said was amassing?"

"I haven't heard any updates." She responded. "I'm not sure if they have sent any scouts to Sipelgas. War records state the Cradesion's home planet was destroyed. There is no information on how much is uninhabitable. From what we have seen now they are quite comfortable underground. Did our allies know that during the war? Or was just the surface destroyed?"

"Fuck I hate these guys." Cullen groaned dropping his head. "I bet you anything the bastards are still there."

* * *

"Who do you think is next?" Cullen whispered as a Cradesion walked towards them, decked out in all its glory.

"Is it going to war?" Adelaide asked, stretching her spasming back.

Stopping in front of Bastion, the thing raised a gun. "It is time."

"Time for what?" Adelaide demanded. There was no response. "Answer me!"

Bastion's cage opened, and he was waved out.

"This doesn't look good," Cullen said.

Bastion hesitated as the Cradesion stepped closer, its four arms waving in agitation.

"Not waiting. Come now," it said.

Bastion glanced over before he leapt for the weapon. They grappled as Adelaide and Cullen yelled encouragements. Its four arms were an advantage Bastion couldn't overcome, no matter how motivated he was. His arms were wrenched behind his back while the gun pointed steadily at his head.

"What are you doing?" Cullen yelled as Bastion was dragged away.

"Damn it. I don't think this is going to end well." Adelaide sank onto the cot, dropping her head into her hands.

Guilt crushed her as she waited for Bastion's return. He was coming back; she refused to believe otherwise. A captain protected her crew—it should have been her taken away.

She glared as a tray of slop was shoved into their cages. The second one of the day, and still no sign of Bastion.

"Why is it so silent?" Cullen demanded.

"I don't know. We're never gone this long in surgery." Adelaide paced around the cage. "Hey! I want to talk with someone." She grabbed the bars, shaking them.

No one responded, so she yelled again.

Cullen watched down the corridor. "I don't think anyone is coming."

"I want answers, damn it." She threw her tray against the bars, where it clanged, the sludge sliding to the floor. "We need to get out of here. We *are* getting out."

Cullen nodded.

"What the urgpar are you crying about?" A Raykar stomped towards them. Its head spikes seemed to straighten more, and their colour brightened.

"I'm not crying! I'm yelling. I demand to have our crewman back." Adelaide clenched her fists, wishing she could have a few minutes with the bastard.

"He's busy." The Raykar somehow smirked at her. His nostrils flared. "What is that stench? Is it fear?"

119

"Not bloody likely. How about we get access to water for cleaning, then maybe we wouldn't stink," Adelaide said, keeping her arms close to her body. She may not be covered in dried, caked blood, but she hadn't cleaned herself since her last gel shower on the Clandestine. The horrors had only been wiped off. "How about you come in here—any smell of fear will come from you." She smirked.

"I. Am. Not. Afraid. Of. A. Human," he stated in English, widening his stance while glared at her.

"You should be. Didn't we slaughter you guys during the war?" Cullen asked, stepping closer to Adelaide's cell.

The Raykar never took his gaze off Adelaide. "You needed help. Otherwise, the spoils would have been ours. We would be stepping on your little bodies."

"How about you prove it?" Adelaide crooked her finger.

The Raykar's spikes flared, but before he could do more than move towards her, a voice yelled out, "No time for this. Leave the food alone. We have plans to complete."

Adelaide glared at the speaker in the hallway. "Where the hell is he?"

"He was not strong enough."

Adelaide's arm shot through the bars, grasping for the creature's laser gun. "What does that mean, you bastard?"

The Raykar stepped back, laughing "You will be next." Then he turned, leaving them alone in silence.

Even if she hadn't known Bastion well, the loss staggered her. He was one of her team, and the enemy destroyed him.

"What's the plan?" Cullen demanded. A crispness clipped his tone, a brisk efficiency that tightened Adelaide's spine. Once they escaped, they would have time to mourn.

Adelaide paced. "Alpha 4 tried to overpower a Cradesion with no luck. I think we'd have better chance with a Raykar. The exoskeleton suits the Cradesions wear are impenetrable without those explosives."

"How do we make it happen?"

"I think we continue to yell out taunts. One of them will eventually come. We know someone is monitoring us, and its common knowledge the Raykar can't control their tempers." She pointed at the speaker.

"Agreed. Monitoring is grunt work. The Cradesions are running the show here."

Adelaide took a few minutes to pull herself together. They were getting out of here now—or they'd die trying.

Soon, both their voices echoed down the hallway taking turns insulting their jailers. Adelaide's voice was hoarse by the time someone decided to grace them with their presence.

"Finally," Adelaide whispered as she tensed in anticipation. The same Raykar came into view. This was going to be easy.

"You are want to die sooner?" he hissed, grabbing the weapon at his waist.

"That was so easy." Adelaide stood up. "So, do the fight with no honour? Afraid to come closer?"

His hand stopped, while his thin lip curled on one side. "I am not afraid." His tongue flicked out. It was unusual, something Adelaide hadn't seen before. The Raykar's gaze shifted around before stepping up to the cage.

"I will defeat you. No one questions my honour."

When her cage opened; Adelaide bent her knees in response. The Raykar would not come out alive. She was getting Cullen out. The Raykar needed to step all the way in so he couldn't change his mind. Cullen edged closer, his hands gripping the bars.

Before advancing, the Raykar ogled her bare legs, then grunted and stepped inside. She kept her eyes trained on him. His torso gave a miniscule twitch before the muscles on his arm rippled. His punch was aimed right at her face. She twisted just in time, grabbing his arm. She knew punching a Raykar probably wouldn't do much damage as their tough, leathery skin was great protection. Her chance lay in the weapon. When she glanced at Cullen, signalling with her eyebrows, the Raykar's claws raked down her arm. Blood seeped out of the shallow wounds.

"Son of a bitch." She grimaced, trying to grapple him while pushing at the same time. Stepping slightly away, Adelaide gained some space. She coiled her muscles, then kicked for all she was worth into his stomach.

The Raykar gave an oomph, stumbling back a couple of steps. She grinned—only a few more. She kept up the kicking, keeping her distance from the deadly claws. He was still able to make contact on her stomach and other arm, but he was closer to where she needed him. Pain radiated from the scratches, her legs threatening to give out. That asshole better not have put poison on his claws—a common practice during the war.

Cullen stretched his hand as far as possible, just shy of the goal. With a grimace, he shook his head.

She gathered her waning strength, pushing it through her leg, the prick teetered towards Cullen's waiting hands. Cullen yanked the weapon from around the Raykar's waist, firing as the Raykar turned. the blast hit his chest armour, punching a hole through to the far wall.

As his body fell, a booming echo reverberated throughout the hull. Adelaide tipped forward, grabbing hold of the bars, gawking at Cullen.

"I don't think your shot damaged the ship to *that* extreme."

Cullen grinned, spinning the weapon around his finger. "I'm good."

Adelaide laughed as red warning lights flashed, coinciding with chittering across the air waves. "Let's get out of here. We need to find Alpha 4, and I want to stop in the torture chamber. Earth could use their tech."

Cullen nodded as Adelaide stumbled out of her cage. She headed to Cullen's, searching for its door release.

"How do I get this open?" She clutched her arm, a couple of drops of blood slipping through her fingers.

"Did he have anything on him?"

"I don't think so."

Adelaide searched the Raykar's body. Nothing. She grabbed his arms, slowly dragging him out sucking the wince back in. A trail of green blood followed them to Cullen's doors. Hoping there was a sensor on him, she pushed him against the bars, but nothing happened.

"Damn it. What the hell is wrong with these assholes? They can't do anything right." Adelaide kicked the motionless body a few times, swearing as she bent her big toe. "Crap, it must release in a control room. Give me the gun. I'll have to search."

Cullen made a face but handed it over through the bars. The ship lurched again, throwing them to the floor.

"I think they're under attack. I'll hurry. Wait here."

"Not going anywhere."

"Sorry," she muttered, hurrying away.

TAURIAN CASSINI
BORN IN 2068; 40 YEARS OLD

OCCUPATION: SMUGGLER
- *Dealt with Adelaide's Brother Dante*

PLANET: RAAU
- *People called the Tu'Val — a warrior race, love to fight and pillage*
- *covered in jungle, warm and humid*
- *species wore very little clothing*
- *Not part of the Mult-Specie Accords*

PHYSICAL DESCRIPTION:
Seven feet tall, light green skin, sculpted body, vivid purple eyes, blond hair to shoulders, and a hairless body. He has a chiseled jawline and defined cheek bones.

WEAPONS:
A long sword strapped to his back and a laser gun strapped to his hip.

PERSONALITY/EMOTIONS:
Strong, entitled, cocky

Chapter 7

Sounds of laser fire, shouting and swearing reached her ears. Adelaide didn't relish meeting anyone on her hunt. Pausing at the corner, she raised the weapon, peering around. Why hadn't anyone come after Cullen shot their comrade? They had to have seen. At the far end, Cradesions scuttled past in their exoskeletons, not seeing her. Sighing in relief, Adelaide continued to wobble towards the first room, where she stopped in front of the door, which didn't open.

"Damn it. The thing is coded to those bastards. Or locked."

She changed the setting on the laser, aimed and fired. She was almost through when the door began sliding. Moving to the side, she waited. A Raykar stuck his head out, her laser made contact blowing it to smithereens. Adelaide grinned, rushing into the empty room. Idiot. She scanned the controls in frustration. What the hell did all the symbols mean? If her translator worked, it would be easy. Figuring the

symbol and picture on the right were for the cells, she
pushed all the buttons, hoping for the best.

Before leaving, she glanced around the room for
anything useful. A black object stuffed in the corner
caught her eye. "Gotcha." Adelaide grinned in triumph.
She'd found her missing fancy super-jacket. What were
the odds? She slipped her arms into the sleeves of the
jacket. "Now we're talking." She didn't care how
ridiculous it appeared over her lovely grey gown.

Where was her sword though? Searching
frantically, she found nothing else. She pushed away
the disappointment, vowing not to leave this ship
without it. One of the last gifts from her brother.
Kicking the remains of the bastard at the door, she
slipped out. The ship lurched again; the halls filled with
smoke. She headed to the cells, running into Cullen
halfway there.

"Thank God," she said, hugging him tight. "Let's
get out of here. We'll check every room we pass for our
missing things." She turned back in the direction she
had come from, hoping that the numbness in her
wounds wasn't a bad sign. At least she could move
easier with the pain reduced.

"We don't have time—what about our other
weapons?" Cullen argued, following her at a run.

"We make time, and the others can be replaced."

They came across another fallen Raykar, and
Adelaide grabbed his weapon, which she handed to
Cullen.

"Who do you think is attacking?" Cullen asked.

"Hopefully allies."

They booted around the corner. She crossed her fingers the escape pods were available and easy enough to find.

Adelaide wished they would turn off the damn alarm. The decibels were going to blow her eardrums if it continued for much longer.

Laser fire flashed across the corridor. Adelaide stopped, causing Cullen to run into her back, propelling her forward. Fighting reverberated throughout the ship. She just wanted to steal a pod and let the two forces kill each other.

"Keep up, Alpha 3." She waved him forward. "Which way?"

"I think we need to go right. Luckily, sounds like less fighting."

"Go, I'll cover you."

With a nod, he scooted ahead of her, his body low to the ground. Adelaide kept watch the other direction until Cullen whistled the all-clear. She took off after him, a blast hitting right behind her.

"Damn it!" She glanced around for the shooter.

Ahead stood an open door with a blaster protruding out. Cullen returned fire as they ran closer, the blaster retreated into the room. Flattening themselves before the doorway, they waited. It was only a few moments before someone roared a challenge and sprang out, shooting.

Diving to the floor, they returned fire. She wasn't quick enough; a shot hit her in the lower leg. Screaming in pain Adelaide, pressed on the wound. A familiar body-type dropped to the floor. The light green skin, bare chest and kilt gave him away.

She swore a blue streak while Cullen regarded her in surprise.

"We have good news and bad news." She groaned, trying to stand up.

"We killed an enemy; isn't that good?" Cullen asked, helping her to her feet.

"The good news is there are the Tu'Val on this ship. The bad is we killed one. We need to lie saying we found him."

Cullen opened and closed his mouth, glancing from the body back to her.

"Okay, we don't have time for an explanation right now. Just take my word for it. We need to find more of them so we can surrender." Adelaide stepped into the room, searching for Bastion and the sword. Nothing. "Those mother fuckers." She spun around, then headed down the hallway.

"I hope you know what you're doing" Cullen followed behind her awkwardly limping form.

"How much farther do you think the med bay is?" Adelaide asked, blood leaving a trail behind her.

"I think it's around the corner to the left."

Reaching the junction, Adelaide braced her hand on the wall, peered around the corned, then quickly pulled back. "Can't go that way." She nodded for Cullen to follow. Leaving a bloody handprint behind, she ran in the opposite direction, Cullen at her side.

"What about the tech?" he gestured behind them.

"We'll come back."

They reached what seemed like the main fighting. Three Cradesions along with a couple of Raykar were battling against about ten Tu'Val. The Cradesions fought with supreme skill and viciousness, holding the Tu'Val back. The turning point came when a crazy-ass Tu'Val bellowed a war cry, raised his long sword and laser and ran between his men right at the enemy. His muscles rippled as he swung the sword, taking the head of the front Raykar. He blocked a laser with his sword, returning fire. He made direct contact with the neck of another Cradesion, dropping him. The rest of the Tu'Val followed, shooting at the remaining enemy.

Adelaide sighed. "Better help save the idiot."

"Don't think he needs it."

"You never know; I might get lucky." She grinned before stepping into the fray, firing above the Tu'Val.

They made short work of the other side. Then the Tu'Val turned their weapons on Adelaide and Cullen.

"Drop your weapons!" a voice yelled.

"We were *helping* you," she growled. "Don't be idiots."

"Are you sure about antagonizing them?" Cullen whispered, lowering his weapon.

Adelaide shook her head. "No." She didn't lower her arms, but the shaking in her legs increased. She didn't like the gazes she received as the warriors noticed her attire.

"Hello, Red," a low, sexy voice said. The man of her dreams and nightmares came into view.

Frowning, she finally lowered her arms. "Taurian. Fancy meeting you here."

"I was not expecting this prize when we boarded." He approached her, motioning at the blood pooling on the floor.

"It's nothing. We've been guests of the Cradesions for a few days. I'm hoping you can take us back."

Taurian tsked, inspecting her for more wounds, poking at the swollen scratch on her arm.

"What the fuck, Taurian." With a glare, Adelaide jerked her arm away. "That hurt!"

"You are fine, and you get to come with us now." He grinned. "As I said, you are my prize for conquering the enemy. Also, we are saving you."

"Not bloody likely. You need to learn how to ask, we rescued ourselves and can just as easy find ourselves some escape pods. Don't need you." Adelaide shoved the butterflies in her stomach down, turning to leave.

Cullen shifted closer to Adelaide, drawing Taurian's fierce glare.

"Who is he?" Taurian demanded.

Adelaide was tempted to poke the bear but decided she didn't want Cullen killed. It appeared Taurian still considered her his.

"None of your business. A crewman," Adelaide and Cullen answered at the same time.

"It's fine, Cullen." She pushed his laser down. "I'll explain later."

Taurian watched the exchange with narrowed purple eyes. Some hair came loose from the tie, falling against his chiseled jawline.

"Let's negotiate once we're off this tub. I need to grab some items on the way." Adelaide shifted the weight on her injured leg.

"All spoils are property of the Tu'Val. My warriors will escort you to our ship."

Two men stepped forward, grabbing their arms.

Adelaide resisted. "We need that tech. It can save a lot of lives. Also, the body of one of my men is on this ship. I want it."

"Yes, it can save lives. For *Tu'Val*. Our king will determine if we share with others." He paused. "If we see this body, I will bring it."

"Bastard! I hate you!" Adelaide screamed, yanking at her arm as they were dragged forward.

Taurian laughed. "I don't think so. Take them; we need to leave."

"Make sure you grab a Cradesion. We need to know how they tick—and find my sword," Adelaide yelled.

Ignoring her, Taurian stalked out of the room.

*　　*　　*

"What's going on?" Cullen demanded as they were led onto Taurian's ship.

"Not here," she hissed, glaring at their escorts as they were divested of their weapons. At least their final destination wasn't the brig, just a small room with a cot.

When their escorts left, Cullen faced her, arms crossed over his chest. "Okay, spill it." He frowned at her.

Sighing, she collapsed on the bed, where she lifted her leg gingerly. "It doesn't matter; he knows who we are. To make a long story short . . ."

"Not bloody likely. I want it all."

"Fine." She huffed, embarrassment filling her. "This past year, my brother got into trouble, and I had to rescue him. Found out he was to do a job for Taurian, who took a shine to me. He's determined I'm going to be his bride."

"You're shitting me!" Cullen said, eyebrows climbing.

When she shook her head, he laughed.

"Oh, that's good. How did you reel him in?"

"Disabled one of his ships and escaped from his planet where I was held hostage. His species value a show of force and strength." Adelaide glared at Cullen's bent over form. "It isn't *that* funny, you bastard."

"Yes, it is. Your fiancé saved us." Tears streamed down his face.

Adelaide explored the area for something to throw.

Cullen must have sensed it because he backed up, his hands out. "Fine, fine. All good."

She grumbled, a small smile on her lips. It had been fun escaping his clutches, other than the man-eating plant in the jungle.

"Who is he? Looked like he was in charge."

"He's the commander of the Raau fleet."

"This gets better and better." Cullen grinned, clapping her shoulder as he sat beside her.

"You really want to end up dead now, after surviving torture?" she threatened.

"Depends."

"On what?"

"If I have to see him courting you." He laughed again.

Adelaide punched his arm with a grin, which quickly faded as she slouched on the bed.

"I think you need a doctor." Cullen eyed the blood pooling on the floor.

"Probably, but I'm too exhausted to do anything."

"I think your fiancé might get pissed if his prize dies." Cullen stood and walked to the door.

Adelaide was surprised when the door swished open. Cullen stuck his head out, yelling, "Hey, you! She needs medical attention."

A stomping noise came from the other side of the wall. A large, gorgeous man walked into view.

"Rjey od rtamh?" he demanded.

Cullen glanced at Adelaide with a question in his eyes.

"See the blood? I need medical," she answered sarcastically shifting her aching leg. Her arms and stomach had stopped bleeding, just a crusted mess.

He gawked at her in surprise. "O rozz dumf e quf nay," he said; then he was gone.

Adelaide shook her head. How on earth had he missed seeing her injuries?

"Why didn't my translator work? What did he say?"

"I'm not sure why not. Maybe because it's an old dialect not spoken any longer. I don't think they speak this around others."

"Why were you able to understand?"

"I learned the language long ago."

"Did he know we might not understand?"

"Likely." She gave a weak smile. "The Tu'Val believe most individuals are weaker and not worthy."

The door slid open, and a med bot glided in. "What is your medical issue?" it asked.

"Where should I start," she said sarcastically. "My leg, my chest, and arm. I'm also in pain."

The bot glided closer, a compartment opening in its middle. One thin white metal arm reached inside, pulling out a stubby rod. When the tip began glowing, the bot ran it over her leg and arm wounds. The hole and scratch sealed. Their tech could heal many life-threatening injuries but couldn't bring someone back to life like the Cradesion's tech—or reattach severed limbs so well.

"Take this."

The bot handed over a pain strip, which she placed on her tongue, sighing in relief. As she pulled up her shirt to reveal her wounded stomach, Cullen turned away with a grimace.

Once the other wounds were cleaned and bandaged, she said, "We both need our feet healed." She lifted hers to display the cut soles.

Cullen shook his head. "I'm fine."

"Sit your ass down and get them checked. You can't tell me they aren't like mine." She scowled.

The bed sank as Cullen sat beside her, lifting his feet as well. They were in the same condition.

After the injection and healing, the bot left.

"So now what?" Cullen asked, focused on the closed door.

"Time to see if our comms work." Adelaide pushed a button, barely keeping the yell in as the holodisplay popped up. "Gil, can you hear me?"

A couple of minutes of silence passed before Gil's concerned face showed. "Where the hell are you? I've been tearing the place apart searching for you. You are never going on a mission without me again!" As he talked, relief filled his eyes, his lips tightening.

"I know." Adelaide closed her eyes, pulling herself together. She could imagine Gil in those cages. Even with their healing in between sessions, Gil wouldn't have made it out.

"We've been rescued. I can't talk now until I get more details. Are the survivors safe?" she demanded, leaning closer to her wrist.

"Yes. Another Earth ship rendezvoused with me to take them to safety."

"Great!" Cullen said. "What about the rest?"

"The rest of what?" Gil asked.

"There's got to be more to the story than we got them to safety." Cullen said.

"We'll discuss everything later," Adelaide said. "We should be getting company soon."

"Wait. Who rescued you?" Gil asked.

Adelaide rolled her eyes as Cullen snorted. "You might be walking her down the aisle soon." He chuckled when Adelaide pushed him off the bed.

Gil's mouth dropped open. "How in the hell did Taurian get you again?"

"It's a long story. Can you get my location?"

"No, you're still shielded."

"I'll send you coordinates where to meet."

"Hurry—I don't have a lot of time."

Before Adelaide could respond, Gil disappeared.

"What did he mean?" she demanded.

"Not sure, but let's find this Taurian." Cullen stood up.

"We'll have to wait. If we push him or make too many demands, it won't go our way."

"So, we just wait." Cullen frowned.

"He should be here soon. He'll want to gloat."

"He has some rights. They defeated a Cradesion ship."

"Yeah, yeah." Adelaide lay down, facing the wall. "I'm going to get some shut eye while I have the chance, if I can."

"Go ahead." Cullen waved his hand as he stood pacing the room.

* * *

Adelaide woke to swearing, a thud and the bed jostling.

"What's going on?" she demanded, opening her eyes.

Taurian stood over Cullen, who was lying prone on the floor. His fists were clenched, his eyes glaring daggers.

"Taurian, what the hell is wrong?" she yelled.

He turned his glower on her. "He was touching you." Though his voice was gruff, he unclenched his fingers.

"Oh, for fuck's sake." She sat up, shuffling to the edge. "I was sleeping! And I can touch anyone I want."

Maybe she shouldn't have said that, as thunder filled Taurian's face. The guards at the door took a step in, making her groan.

"What did you expect? We were put in a room with one bed."

"Not to sleep together!"

"We've been tortured for four days, haven't had a good meal in all that time and we stink!" By the end of her speech Adelaide was almost yelling. She stepped over Cullen who had wisely stayed prone, fisted her hands on her hips.

Taurian, releasing a deep breath, caressed her cheek, then motioned for the guards. Adelaide opened her lips to protest but slammed them shut when he said, "Take them to be cleansed and given proper food. I will find you later." Taurian gave her one last ogle filled with promise—or a threat, in her opinion—before leaving the room.

She shook herself. "Hey! What's happening? Did you find Bastion?" Adelaide yelled. No response came as they were ushered out of the room. She growled in frustration. It was essential for Adelaide to rendezvous with Gil and find out what the hell happened. There was no way they were galivanting about space with Taurian.

*   *   *

Despite having to use cleansing gel instead of water, Adelaide felt a hundred percent better. Most ships didn't use water any longer, not since the gel was developed. Squeaky clean, Adelaide riffled through the cabinet yanking out a shirt and pants closest to her size. She made a face as she tugged them on without any underwear—not the most comfortable thing. Next came the socks, followed by heaven. They weren't her boots, but with two pairs of socks for comfort, she couldn't complain.

The guards and Cullen were waiting outside the room.

"Feel better?" Cullen asked with a grin.

"Getting there. Once I have food in my belly, I'll be ready to fight."

Entering the mess hall, Adelaide strode directly to the replicator, where she punched in her request. Grinning, she carried her tray to an empty table and dug in, moaning in delight. She actually had to chew, something she wouldn't be complaining about. Cullen plopped next to her, laughing.

"What?" she demanded.

"Look around."

Adelaide's eyes widened as she took in the other occupants. All of them were eyeing her with hunger on their faces.

"Your moaning was quite loud." Cullen's laughter increased as her face reddened.

"It's good food," she said defensively, shovelling more in. Cullen grinned, following suit.

"Where's Taurian?" Adelaide asked one of their guards as she finished her food.

He glanced at her with a frown.

"I need to speak with him; it's urgent."

"The *commander* is busy." He stressed Taurian's title turning away.

Adelaide stood. "Unless you want me wandering where I shouldn't be, take me to him now." Adelaide crossed her arms, glaring at him, wishing for her weapons. The Tu'Val usually only responded to force, which got them more excited.

Cullen stood next to her, his body stiffening as the other men turned to watch. That's right—all men. The Tu'Val women may be as fierce as the men, but you wouldn't find them on one of their ships. They stayed planet-side, safe from other species. Never underestimate the women though, because little girls trained right along with the boys. But from what Adelaide understood, the women on the planet liked to be pampered only fighting if their planet was threatened.

The guard growled at Adelaide, checked his comm, then walked to the door.

"Let's go," Adelaide told Cullen, following.

They were led around the ship, eventually ending up on the magnificent bridge. Seven others sat at the navigation and tactical stations. Taurian lounged in a highbacked chair edged with what appeared to be emeronze. It couldn't be—Adelaide shook her head in wonder, telling herself not to gawp. There was no way she wanted Taurian to know his ship impressed her. The more Adelaide inspected her surroundings the more Emeronze she spotted. Emeronze was one of the rarest metals in the galaxy, this ship had it in spades.

"Red. Enjoying the view?" Taurian asked with a grin.

Adelaide crossed her arms and tried glaring in his direction. She wasn't sure if she accomplished that the task. A stupid smile was fighting to break free. Damn it, he was growing on her. This could cause problems in the future.

"I need coordinates to send to Gil where he can pick us up."

"We do not have time." Taurian spun around, punching buttons on his arm rest.

"What do you mean? You can't keep us here." Adelaide stepped towards him but stopped immediately when two Tu'Val raised their weapons at her. She scanned around, tensing her body preparing to dive. Taurian waved his hand.

"Put them down; she will not harm me."

The warriors regarded her suspiciously then eyed Taurian.

"Now!" he yelled.

Cullen twitched.

Adelaide couldn't stop herself from asking, "How do you know I won't?"

Taurian glanced at her with a smug grin, his eyes twinkling.

The bastard was right, but sure as shit she wouldn't admit it. Stepping back, bracing her feet, Adelaide glowered at him. "And why don't we have time?"

"The trail is growing cold."

"What trail?" she demanded, throwing her hands in the air. It was like pulling teeth, it was difficult to ignore the other hulking men in the room glaring in her direction. Probably thinking how dare she speak to the commander this way.

"Not that a commander needs to explain anything to you." Taurian's eyes hardened. "But this once. We were tracking two Cradesion vessels. When they split from each other, we attacked."

"Can you at least tell me what direction we are travelling so I can inform Gil?" Adelaide asked, knowing her toe was almost across the line. The Tu'Val didn't accept anyone challenging their commander. It was a sign of disrespect. She didn't mean for it to come across as that, but Adelaide was used to being in charge. All information came to her, and final decisions were from her mouth. Ceding to someone else was difficult, to Taurian even more so.

"I will send you the information."

When Adelaide's wrist comm beeped, she nodded her thanks. "Did you find the body of our crewman?"

"We might have. The body is in the med bay."

"We want to see it." Adelaide struggled to keep her voice calm and non-demanding as Cullen nodded at her side.

"The guards will escort you." He waved his hand, dismissing them.

"Is there any place off limits?" she asked him, glancing back at Cullen. He stood rigid turned slightly away from her, watching the peanut gallery.

"The guards will indicate if you are to leave." Taurian didn't lift his head from the map displayed.

"Fine." Adelaide spun around, motioning Cullen to follow. "Let's explore," she whispered.

Cullen nodded, leaving the bridge after her.

Adelaide glared at their guards. "Bring us too medical?"

She stomped off behind them, bracing herself for what they would discover. As Adelaide followed the guards, she forwarded the coordinates to Gil.

The guards stopped in front of a set of double doors, motioning her forward.

Stepping into the room, Adelaide spotted the doctor sitting at a desk. Two bodies lay on exam tables against the far wall.

"What are you doing in here?" The doctor stood.

"We're here to see our crewman." Adelaide gestured at the human body as she glared at the Cradesion.

"I'm not sure you want to see." His eyes filled with pity.

"We need to know." Cullen strode forward with Adelaide following.

She ran into Cullen's back when he came to an abrupt halt, gasping. Adelaide walked around his stiff body and viewed what remained of Bastion. She had no idea what had done the damage, but they would pay. There was no way he hadn't felt everything. His chest was shredded; stab wounds littered his body. A hole stared back at her where his left eye should have been, and large gaping cuts ran the length of his face. Both ears were missing. Tears filled her eyes as Cullen gagged beside her.

"What the hell did they do this for?" Cullen snarled, staggering forward. He reached towards the body then dropped his hand.

"I don't know, but we will destroy them." Adelaide turned to the doctor. "We want to release his body."

"You will need to talk with the commander. I will try to clean it up as best as I can."

Adelaide nodded before walking out of the room. "I need to speak with the commander."

"He's busy," one guard answered with a snarl.

"When will he be unbusy?" she asked, clenching her fists.

The guard shrugged. "The commander will speak with you when he has finished his duties."

When Cullen growled, Adelaide grabbed his arm, shaking her head slightly. Turning, she led the way down the corridor. "Let's explore until we can get answers."

The two guards stalked behind them, their steps echoing in the silence. Adelaide walked around the large ship to get her bearings. If something happened, she didn't want to be stuck. They passed the mess hall, holodeck, gym and living quarters. The only place barred to them was the engine room. Adelaide couldn't believe how she had missed all the Emeronze throughout the ship. Not as extreme as the bridge, but she saw the dark-green glow the metal emitted. Adelaide was surprised how well the metal colour complimented the Tu'Val's light green skin. She wasn't sure how the metal produced the faint light, but once it was mined and smelted, the metal turned a gorgeous green.

The ore, found deep in a meteor's core. Many miners were killed as lethal chemicals were emitted from the core during extraction. But once it was heated and separated, it was no longer deadly. The price for Emeronze continued to rise as the mining still killed many no matter the precautions taken. The metal didn't just glow but was one of the strongest materials known. Not even laser fire did anything to it. Of course, with its limited supply, the Tu'Val decided to use the precious metal as decoration.

Adelaide needed to expel some of the restless energy coursing through her body before she did or said something stupid, like marching onto the bridge and punching Taurian in the face. "Let's go beat on each other," she said.

Cullen flashed a humourless smile. "Sounds good."

Stepping into the large room, she was impressed with the array of weapons lining the wall. Nets and poles hung from the thirty-foot ceiling, while matts covered half the floor space.

"What are those for?" she asked their guards.

They both smirked. "Training."

Adelaide grumbled; they must take lessons from Taurian, giving the least amount of information as possible. She'd need to come back when others were training—she could guess but really wanted to see it being used. Adelaide strode to the middle of the matts and stood with her eyes closed. Taking deep breaths, she let the tension fall away before slowly moving. The motions came easily as she flowed through her katas to warm up her stiff muscles. Having so much room was a treat. She'd never had this much.

Though Adelaide had learned from the best, achieving her third-degree black belt was no easy feat. It required years of training, pain and broken body parts. If you couldn't fight through it, her sensei believed, then mastery wasn't possible. Of course, at her age, it seemed her body hurt a lot quicker, lasting longer. As her limbs loosened, a smile pulled at her lips, her mind calming.

Completing the final move, she opened her eyes searching around for Cullen. What she found was the guards gaping at her with their jaws slack. *Oh, come on.* They had to start bringing their women on flights with them if her warm-up exercises turned them cross-eyed.

Ignoring them, she turned to Cullen. "You ready?" she called.

"Sure, but watching you, I'll probably get my ass kicked." He hung up a practice sword he'd been swinging around and sauntered to her.

"I'll go easy." She grinned, bending her knees, her eyes tracking his movements.

They circled each other, searching for openings or weaknesses. Cullen jumped forward, his tight fist aiming at her solar plexes. Adelaide stepped to the right, thrusting her hands down, latching onto his arm. Using her hips with his forward motion, Adelaide flung him past her body.

Cullen curled his form, rolling back to his feet, spinning around, throwing his hands up to his face.

Adelaide grinned. "Not bad, just too slow."

Cullen snorted. "Keep talking, woman. Getting cocky is a detriment."

"It's not cocky if I can back it." Laughing, she threw kicks at Cullen's left side, which he blocked with a wince.

They fought fast and furious, neither one giving an inch. Until Adelaide noticed a small opening on Cullen's left side. She placed a well-aimed jab, and as he bent forward slightly, her elbow met his nose. Cullen swore as Adelaide grabbed his arm, throwing her hip. He flew over, landing on his back. *No rolling for him this time*, she thought smugly.

"I give," Cullen wheezed out, his eyes closed.

Adelaide grinned, falling beside him. "Good workout." Sweat pooled beneath her body. *Gross.*

"Yeah, yeah. Were you just playing with me?" He turned his head slightly, glaring at her.

"No. Not really."

He grunted, heaving his body up. "I'm going for a shower, then collapsing. You stay away from me until you hear from Taurian."

She laughed as he limped to the guards waiting at the door. For a time, she had forgotten about them, but now her frown returned. Time to clean up before contacting Gil.

Chapter 8

Adelaide sat on the small bed in her private room. She liked Cullen, but not *that* well. Pressing buttons on her comm, Adelaide waited for a response.

"Where are you?" Gil demanded his face showing on the holodisplay. From his surroundings, it appeared he was still on Clandestine's bridge, which was a good sign.

"I'm not sure. We're in pursuit of another Cradesion ship. Taurian hasn't deigned to speak with me yet. All he's said is no rendezvous right now. I did send you the direction we're travelling in—you can follow with the coordinates of the ship they destroyed.

"They were able to destroy one of their ships?" Gil sounded amazed.

"What's going on, Gil?" she asked. "Are you hurt?"

"No. I was able to contact Earth, they took the survivors."

"Were you able to get the collars off?"

"No, though the med bots on board here were able to stabilize them. Hopefully the Syndicate has the ability."

"What about the planet?" It must be all men, Adelaide grumbled to herself. Least amount of info as possible. "Tell me the story, man."

Gil shifted on the screen, sighed scraping his hand over his jawline. "Once I beamed as many survivors as possible, I escaped the planet, engaged cloaking and waited in the debris field to hear from you. It got too dicey to wait any longer because a couple of Cradesion ships came into orbit. So, we used the jump gate to escape."

"Was Earth sending any ships back to the planet?"

"I'm not sure. We never got that far in the debriefing."

"What do you mean?" she asked suspiciously.

"I left."

"What! You'll be court marshalled."

"Don't care," he growled. "They refused to launch a search and rescue for you three. I was expected to head back to Earth. Not bloody likely."

Warmth filled Adelaide along with dread. What would the military do to him? He'd stolen a prototype ship.

"Thanks, Gil. How are you able to pilot the ship by yourself?" Adelaide narrowed her eyes at his image.

"Picked up some friends." He grinned.

"For fuck's sake, Gil, you have non-military personnel on a prototype ship. What were you thinking?" she yelled.

"Rescuing you," he said quietly, shutting her up. "I was only on this mission because of you—I'm not abandoning you. Now, tell me how you got rescued by Douchebag."

Adelaide smirked but it didn't last as her story progressed.

*　　*　　*

Adelaide jerked awake, a scream erupting from her mouth. Eyes wide open in fright, she gathered her bearings. Her head swivelled while the dark froze her body on the bed. Breathing deeply, Adelaide slowed her heartbeat so it didn't feel like her chest was going to burst. Slowly, her mind pieced together the last day and she was able to calm herself, she was safe. She'd take Taurian's harassment any day of the week over torture and captivity. Not that it said much. Closing her eyes and taking a deep breath, Adelaide tried purging the view of Gil being tortured. Her mind produced some fucked up shit. She would never feel guilt about sending Gil with the survivors to save him from the cradesions. He was a grown ass man and could beat her until kingdom come, but she would always protect him. Some of her fondest memories were tinkering with Gil in the engine room to avoid her brother. Eventually it became her safe space.

Grumbling, Adelaide swung her legs over the side of the bed, setting her bare feet on the cold floor. Sweat dripped down her back under the shirt she wore. The coolness of the ground worked its way slowly up her legs. Moving to the cupboard, she removed her top, throwing it on the floor. She pulled another on, shuddering at the memory of her torture. Her skin flared with remembered pain.

After one of the sessions with their captors it was all, she could do to keep her clothes on. Anything touching her skin hurt like the devil.

"It's not real; it's not real," she chanted, rubbing her arms, proof she was alive and intact. Her comm showed she'd actually slept most of the night. Only a few hours remained till breakfast. Maybe she'd check to see if anyone was working out. Her body was stiff but was slowly becoming hers again.

Adelaide was surprised no guards stood in the hallway. Maybe they thought she'd sleep in. After verifying she was alone, she strode hopefully in the direction of the gym. Yesterday, she had still been exhausted mentally and physically.

As she drew close, the sounds of fighting and yelling drifted towards her. She grinned. Watching the Tu'Val train would be a treat. They were warriors through and through. With their strength and speed, none were willing to give an inch. When Adelaide stepped into the room, everyone came to an abrupt halt, staring in her direction. The scrutiny was mostly curious, but she took note of several, knowing she'd have to watch her back.

"Don't worry about me; keep going." She waved her hands with a grin. The Tu'Val turned back, ignoring her as she leaned against the wall to observe. A few occasionally glanced her way, but for the most part she was left in peace.

Adelaide glanced up and couldn't contain her gasp. *Holy shit.*

One guy swung from pole to pole, landing on the nets before climbing up to another obstacle with no safety net.

"What do you think, Red?" a whisper in her ear made Adelaide jump.

How did he sneak up on her? She glared up at Taurian, trying not to check out his defined chest. But it was difficult as a few beads of sweat slid down to the low-riding pants. At least they weren't wearing their kilts up there. That would be a sight she wouldn't want to see.

"Interesting." She shrugged nonchalantly. "Looks pretty easy." Adelaide swore in her head, trying to keep her expression impassive.

"Really." Taurian smirked. "How about a little wager, then?"

She groaned. "I've never done it before; I'd be at a disadvantage."

"Oh, come on, Red. You said it looks easy, and I have seen your fight moves. Or do you want to concede I am better."

Taurian leaned closer, placing one hand on the wall by her head. Everyone had stopped and was watching them. She couldn't get out of it. Damn her big mouth.

"Fine, what's the wager?" she demanded.

He leaned farther in until his lips were right in front of hers. She was very tempted to move the couple of inches to make contact. Taurian grinned, a twinkle in his eye, probably figured out her thoughts.

"If I win, you will stay on my ship. If you win, I will let Gil take you away until another time."

Adelaide considered him, trying to determine if he was joking. She knew Tu'Vals wouldn't lie or squelch on a bet. It would go against their code of honour, but she didn't like the "until another time" he tacked on.

"Fine." She smiled. Against his bulk, her smaller stature should help. When younger, training for her karate had been similar, no problem.

"Let's shake on it." She held out her hand.

"I have got something better."

Before she could move, Taurian grabbed the back of her head, pressing his lips to hers. The kiss was slow and sensual. He pulled back, his eyes never leaving her face.

Adelaide ignored the hoots from the peanut gallery. "I hope you don't seal all your deals that way." She breathlessly stepping away, a little unsteadily.

"Only you, Red." Taurian followed, steps behind her, to the starting point.

"Should I go easy on you? Wouldn't want your human body to be damaged." Taurian ran his gaze slowly down the length of her frame, causing shivers over her body.

"Don't worry yourself about little old me." Adelaide pushed him aside, eyeing the first rung. Even with her height she'd still need to spring up in order to grab the rings on the wall. Taurian's seven feet gave him a huge reach advantage.

Pointing at the course, Taurian asked, "Do you see the path? We will start when signalled. The first one to make it to the other side wins."

Adelaide nodded, studying the course. She had no plans to stay on this ship—time to get back to hers. Bending her knees, Adelaide waited for the signal, then surged upwards with Taurian right beside her. Her finger tips just reached the rings, she gripped tight, using her toes on the wall to propel her body up, stretching for the next pole with one hand. Once positioned for the first leap, she flung her body across the open expanse. Adelaide really wanted to close her eyes, but she needed to see the coming pole to grasp. Using her momentum, she spun around the pole until her feet could land on top and she balanced, examining the next target, a net. Pushing off with her feet, Adelaide smacked into the wall but hung onto the net with sheer will.

Taurian was one obstacle ahead. She needed to step it up. Hand over fist, she scaled to the top, placing her hands into the wall grooves above. Each obstacle Adelaide made it through, she gained on him. The noises of approval or denial could be heard from below. Adelaide tuned them out, pushing her body and passing Taurian with a grin.

He grunted in response, swinging his strong body from pole to pole. Triumph filled her as they descended to the finish line. She was going home!

"No!" she yelled as Taurian released his hold from the net above her, dropping twenty feet to pass her. He landed on both feet, rolling into a somersault and back up.

Adelaide finished, landing close to his upright body. "What the hell was that?" she demanded, ignoring the cheering.

Taurian grinned. "You were worried about me?"

"Never." She punched him in the arm.

"A Tu'Val can survive a fall greater than that," a warrior answered, glaring at her.

Taurian looked insulted by her insinuations.

She noticed Cullen standing close to the door and strode towards him.

"Do not forget I win, Red," Taurian called after her.

Adelaide stuck her middle finger up didn't turning around. *He should know the meaning*, she thought. Many of the spectator's congratulated her on the course, making her smile. Taurian's laughter followed her out of the room.

"That was amazing," Cullen commented, trying to keep up with her "What does he win?"

Adelaide started swearing, then muttered under her breath.

"What did you say?" he demanded stepping in front of her.

"If he won, we stayed on his ship."

"What the hell! We have to get back to command." He started pacing. "You plan to go AWOL?"

"No," she hissed, shaking her head. "Taurian doesn't know I'm back in the military."

"Then why did you agree?"

"If I didn't, we would probably be locked up; we'd learn nothing. This way, we can pass on information to the brass. It's not like I can force him to release us."

"This is going to blow up in our faces." Cullen sighed. "What's the status on Gil?"

They stopped in front of Adelaide's room.

"He's AWOL. The brass decided not to send a rescue team for us, Gil took offense to that."

Cullen gawped at her with disbelief. "So, where is he?"

"Heading our way now. He was returning to Tikaani before I contacted him."

"This isn't good." Cullen shook his head. "I'm assuming he has the Clandestine, Earth's prototype ship. They won't let him go."

"I know. I'll contact the general—leave it to me. I'll see you later." Adelaide stepped into her room, waving goodbye to him.

*   *   *

Sitting up on her bed, Adelaide rubbed her sore eyes. At least her exhaustion levels were down. Before she could change her mind, she hit her comm. "Taurian we need to talk," she demanded.

"What took you so long?" Taurian grinned. "I am on the bridge."

"Somewhere private."

"Meet me here," he said, then disconnected.

"Damn it." She hit her comm button again. "Cullen, we're going to the bridge."

"I'll be waiting."

Adelaide finished dressing, then stepped out into the corridor. Cullen waited there.

"Did you learn anything?" he asked, falling into step with her.

"No." She glared back, seeing one of their shadows. "Where's the other?" She gestured with her head.

"No idea," Cullen said.

When they stepped onto the bridge, Taurian motioned them to follow him into his ready room. As soon as the door closed, Adelaide confronted Taurian.

"What the hell is going on?" she demanded.

"Sit down." Taurian indicated the chairs in front of the desk.

Adelaide stepped around the table stopping suddenly, her heart beating a mile a minute. Blinking back the tears she reached with trembling fingers. "You found it." Her voice hushed.

Taurian gave a small smile. "Of course. I would do anything for you."

Adelaide lifted the sword, a smile on her lips. There wasn't a speck on it, and the edge had been sharpened. "How am I supposed to yell at you now?" she joked.

Taurian shrugged watching her in silence as she sat with the sword in her lap.

"We were heading out to Tikaani when we spotted the two Cradesion ships and followed."

"Weren't they cloaked?" Cullen asked in surprise.

Taurian eyed Cullen like he was a cockroach. Not liking the reaction, Adelaide glared at Taurian, tapping her fingers on the armchair.

Taurian glanced in her direction. "No. They were leaving the planet and we were able to lock onto their signatures to follow."

"What is the plan when you reach this second ship?" she asked.

"Kill them, of course."

"I want in," she stated, sitting forward.

"Me too." Cullen crossed his arms.

Taurian considered them both before saying, "Fine, but if he dies—not my problem."

Cullen snarled. Adelaide placed a restraining hand on his arm, removing it quickly when Taurian glared at their joining.

Men, she thought in disgust. "Is your doctor examining the Cradesion you brought on board?" she asked as a distraction.

"Yes, he is examining it right now."

"I want to observe. See how these bastard's tick."

"You are quite demanding when you have no leverage."

Adelaide shrugged. "Meh, might as well ask for the moon."

Taurian gave her a strange look. "You can go to medical. The crew was impressed with you today." He leaned back in his chair, smiling at her.

"Why? I didn't win."

"No. But there have not been any humans to pass the gauntlet before, so quickly. I only won by dropping."

Adelaide gawked at him. Had he deigned to give her a compliment? She needed to document it. What was he planning—why was he being so nice?

She narrowed her eyes. "We would like to release Bastion to his home world," she stated.

"Once the battle is over." Taurian nodded.

"When do you expect to intercept?" Cullen asked.

"Soon."

"You're not going to trail the ship back to the main force?" Adelaide asked, her brows lifting. "Maybe they are going to their home planet. Or settled on a new one."

"Our purpose is to seek and destroy. With just a couple of our ships, we can't defeat their whole force."

"But you can send intel back," she said.

"We will continue forward, but we have others out there, tracking their movements."

She straightened. "What have you found out?"

"We do not share." Taurian stood, crossing his arms over his wide chest.

As his muscles rippled, Adelaide tried not to stare, failed completely, and glared instead. "Damn it, Taurian. We need to work together."

"Not with Earth. Now, I have things to do."

Adelaide pushed back her chair. "What about weapons and better clothes?" She lifted the loose shirt away from her body with disgust.

"You can use the replicator in the med bay when you are there. I will supply you with weapons when we leave." Taurian opened the cupboard. "I found this for you to use until you can have one made." He held out a scabbard.

"I'm speechless." She reached out her hand.

"That is amazing." Taurian laughed.

"Now I'm not." Adelaide frowned, grabbing the present. "Thanks." Adelaide stomped out of the room without a backward glance, Cullen's footfalls echoing hers.

"I'm astounded we'll have weapons," he said when they were on their own.

"Oh, we won't have them for long."

"What?"

"We won't be allowed to keep them on his ship, just the Cradesion's."

Cullen muttered as they walked. She tried not to grin, sure she heard him complaining about losing his babies, et cetera. "Your original babies are lost, but you can adopt some new ones. Maybe the Tu'Val will have more powerful weapons you can keep."

"You think?" his eyes lit up, a smile stretching his lips.

Adelaide laughed, "Nope. But don't stop hoping for a miracle."

"You're really mean." Cullen punched her arm. "Have you tried to contact HQ?" he asked, stopping at the med bay doors.

"I will after this."

"Are you avoiding them?"

"Maybe." She sighed. "I'm not sure what to do about Gil. Turning him in isn't an option."

Cullen nodded.

The med door opened for them, and Adelaide wrinkled her nose as a putrid smell wafted out.

"What the hell?" Cullen grumbled, covering his nose.

Dread filled Adelaide; she didn't want to see their comrade. When they stepped into the room, she sighed with relief: only the headless Cradesion lay on the exam table. Bastion was nowhere in sight. The Tu'Val doctor, bent over the body, turned to them with a frown.

"Taurian said we could be here."

"I know." He focused again on the cadaver. After using a laser to cut through the exoskeleton, the doctor grabbed a tool to pry it open, revealing the little four-foot body.

Adelaide wondered how such a small creature could cause so much destruction "Have you analyzed the armour yet?" she asked, pointing to the exoskeleton.

"No."

Adelaide and Cullen helped the doctor pull it away from the body, laying it on the floor once fully separated. Her fingers itched to grab a piece and tuck it under her clothes, stealing it away to examine later. She didn't completely trust Taurian to share all the information. Shaking her head, she heaved a sigh. The Tu'Val people always came first, their loyalty to their own unwavering. Adelaide had never heard of one instant where this wasn't the case.

The doctor slowly cut open the creature's body cavity. It was fascinating seeing the inner workings of the enemy; she approached the table. Its four arms lay still on the table. The long thin fingers that used to hold a laser were clenched even in death. Adelaide had never been good at anatomy for humans let alone an alien species. To her, one organ was the same as another. The doctor dictated his findings while his hands lifted organ after organ out of the black body. Cullen gagged behind her as the smell intensified.

"Are they much different than us?" Adelaide asked the doctor during one of his lulls.

He glanced up. "Their organs are slightly smaller and in different locations. Until the autopsy is complete, I won't know for sure, but I believe they don't have as many as a human."

Adelaide leaned in closer, not wanting to miss how to kill them easier.

Cullen tapped on her shoulder. "I think I'm ready to leave."

Adelaide smirked. "What's wrong? The smell isn't so bad." It was hard, but she held back from wrinkling her nose.

Cullen's face was green, and he pursed his lips. "I'll leave this to you." He took a step back.

"That's fine. I've seen enough. Thanks, Doctor."

Cullen hurried ahead of Adelaide as they took their leave of the operating area, heading to the replicator for better clothing.

"I'll put these on in my quarters; I need to contact HQ." Adelaide waved as she left the med bay.

"Do you want me there?"

"No, it might be better if you're not."

"Okay. Let me know our orders."

She nodded. Trepidation filled her as Cullen walked away. She would defend Gil to the end. He had defended her while growing up; her gangly body hadn't been made for fighting back. Everything changed when Gil introduced her to martial arts.

When she was situated, she tugged her hair back, took a deep breath and hit her comm button. "This is Captain Adelaide."

"Patching you through to the general."

Adelaide paced the small area beside her bed, biting her nail, she didn't want to deal with this right now.

"Captain." The stern face of the general came into view. "I'm glad your still with us."

"Thank you, General. As am I. Did the survivors make it?" Adelaide kept her face blank, waiting for a response.

"Yes. Good work, Captain. You and Gil must return to base now." A sound close to a snarl lifted his lips before he shifted, his face smoothing.

Ah shit. "I'm sorry, General, but I haven't been in contact with Gil. I assumed he would be back on Earth."

The general's brows furrowed. "Where are you, Captain?"

"I am on Commander Taurian's ship."

"What?"

"I will be sending a complete report within the next Earth hour. Where is Gil, General? What happened?"

"A ship rendezvoused with the survivors, taking them on board. Gil was ordered to fly directly back to Earth, but there has been no contact with him; he's AWOL."

Adelaide tried to appear shocked. "I'm sure something must have happened. He wouldn't have disobeyed a direct order. What about Tikaani? Why wasn't he sent there to rescue us? Have more ships been sent?"

The general locked eyes with her. It felt like he was trying to pull her apart, but she wouldn't give. "Gil was needed elsewhere with our prototype ship. More ships had been dispatched, but nothing was there. The planet is abandoned."

"Any equipment? That cavern had been full." Her mind cranked.

"Everything was gone. No other survivors."

Damn it, Adelaide thought. Maybe they were on the ship Taurian was pursuing. She had to get off the comm with the general.

"I'll send the report right away." Adelaide's finger was close, but not quick enough.

"I want you on the next transport to Earth. That's an order, Captain. And if you hear from Gil, he better be accompanying you, with the other survivors" The screen blanked.

"Bloody hell." She gave a snarl. It was more satisfying to swear in an alien language. *What did the general mean about other survivors?*

First, she needed to finish her report stating staying with the Tu'Vals would be an advantage to Earth. Then, talking with Gil again.

Chapter 9

After hitting "send," Adelaide stretched her arms above her head, twisting her neck. She grimaced at the popping sounded. The general wasn't going to be pleased with her statement, staying with Commander Taurian would be better for Earth; she expected a call within the next half hour.

"Gil, we need to talk."

It took a minute for the connection.

"Finally, Adelaide," Gil said.

She didn't like how exhausted he looked, and Gil never called her by name.

"What's wrong?" she demanded.

"Nothing." He swiped a hand across his face.

"Don't give me that bullshit. You're in a lot of trouble. Are you having issues with your crew? Isn't the military tracking you? What was the general talking about when he said survivors were missing? Did you discover more?"

Gil looked surprised. "The only problems I'm having with the crew is when they take all my money. I found the tracking device and disabled it."

"So," Adelaide hedged, "We both might be court marshalled right away." She sighed. "Why are you evading my questions?"

"I don't want to discuss on an open channel. What did you do?"

Adelaide was worried. What would be so bad? Also why was he so intrigued? She felt insulted. Most the times she got into trouble wasn't because of her.

"I sent the general my report, telling him we haven't been in contact and I wasn't coming back yet after ordered to return. I think sticking with Taurian will produce relevant information for the war coming. We all know it is."

Gil grinned. "Good for you. I'll stay on this course for now. Let me know if there are any changes."

Her comm flashed with an incoming message. "The general is calling; I'll talk to you later."

An angry general faced Adelaide when she connected. "General."

"Are you saying you're planning to ignore a direct order?" His eye twitched.

Adelaide flinched. *That was new.* "I don't want to, General. But we need to be here when the Cradesion ship is intercepted. The Tu'Val won't share their findings with Earth. With me here, I can get firsthand knowledge to keep Earth informed. Also, Taurian will not detour to drop me off; he doesn't care about our military or making them happy." Adelaide tried to keep her voice calm and not call the general a dumbass.

"I've spoken to Earth Command. They want you back. The Tu'Val aren't part of the Syndicate, therefore we're not working with them."

"General, you haven't seen this enemy. We're going to need all the help we can get, or we will all be destroyed." Adelaide knew in her bones this would be the case. "What did the Syndicate say?"

"They don't have a say on how Earth runs their military," the general scoffed, glaring at her.

"But this affects the whole Syndicate. I need to be here, if I need to go to them, I will."

"Are you threatening me, Captain? You won't like the results."

"I really don't want to, General, but this is too crucial. We might not get another chance. They were able to take down one of their ships."

"I want constant reports. Filter all information to me until I have confirmation from the Syndicate."

"Yes sir."

"And, Captain, when you speak with Gil next, inform him he will be disciplined when this is over."

"Yes sir."

"General out."

Sighing in relief, Adelaide sank into her chair, where she messaged Gil with an update, informing him to continue their course until otherwise detoured.

After grabbing clean clothes, Adelaide headed to the showers.

* * *

Adelaide pulled on her new black pants over lovely underwear. Next came the scabbard across her chest, which she slid her sword into to rest on her back. A message buzzed on her comm to meet in the cargo bay. Grinning, she headed over, having trouble keeping her stride slow. Turning the last corner, she spotted Cullen hurrying her way.

"Time to suit up." Cullen rubbed his hands together, flashing his teeth. "What kind of weapons do you think we'll get?"

"A laser gun."

He frowned. "There has to be more."

Adelaide's lips twitched as she pushed through the gathering Tu'Val soldiers approaching Taurian, who was bellowing orders.

"Red, get over here," he demanded.

With a shrug to Cullen, she stepped over to him. "What weapons do you have?" she asked.

Taurian gestured to the open cabinet behind him. Cullen pushed beside Adelaide, peering around Taurian.

"Hot damn!" He grinned.

Taurian shifted, blocking Cullen's view. "Red, come choose." He ignored Cullen.

Adelaide moved in front, analyzing the different guns, swords and knives.

"Do you have any holsters?" she asked, never looking away.

A black, thin double holster was shoved in her face. She grunted, taking it and strapping around her hips. She reached inside for two medium-sized laser guns shoving them into place.

"Hurry up, Adelaide," Cullen said, shifting behind her.

"Fine, fine." She grabbed a couple of knives strapping their sheaves to her thighs. "Go ahead." She waved him forward getting quickly out of the way as he advanced.

Taurian shoved a mask at Cullen, then stepped into Adelaide's personal space with a smirk.

"Allow me," he said, attaching the mask at her waist, dragging a finger across her stomach.

Adelaide couldn't stop the shivers quickly taking a step back.

"Thanks," she muttered.

Cullen was loading up when the ship pitched sideways, she weaved on her feet.

"Status!" Taurian yelled.

"They're coming about," a voice said over the comms.

"Remember just disable," Taurian ordered.

The ship shuddered; warning signals blared. They pitched again, causing her to fall against Taurian's hard body. His arms wrapped around her, holding her steady. A few of the soldiers cursed, stumbling while trying to keep upright.

"Get ready, men," Taurian yelled over the noise.

They all stood tense, watching the hatch located close to the cargo bay doors.

Cullen stepped closer to Adelaide, whispering, "Have you heard from Gil?"

"I sent him a message. He hasn't responded." She shrugged her shoulder.

Taurian furrowed his brows at them. In response, Adelaide grinned at him, turning her back. His growl made her chuckle while Cullen raised a questioning brow.

"What? It's nothing." She waved her hand.

"Commander, an unknown ship has appeared and is hailing."

"Who the hell is it?" Taurian snarled.

"Maybe it's Gil," Adelaide whispered.

"This is the Clandestine, Captain Gil here. Would you like some assistance?"

"Yes!" Adelaide crowed, raising her fist in glee. The occupants all turned eyeing her.

"This is Commander Taurian. Hold your position. We will be infiltrating the enemy ship. If we require assistance, you will be notified. Commander out." Taurian glared in Adelaide's direction.

She shrugged anticipation ran through her vibrating body as she stared through the tall, muscled bodies blocking her access to the hatch. The ship shuddered. A loud click echoed in the cargo bay. Taurian yelled, sword raised. The others answered the call, a feral grin on all their faces. Even Cullen responded to all the testosterone filing the bay.

"Open the hatch," Taurian called, pushing to the front, stepping first into the connecting tunnel. He waited until more warriors filled the space before entering a code into the keypad on the door. It slid open revealing, the outer hull of the Cradesion ship.

Adelaide's mouth dropped open as Taurian's sword began glowing a soft purple before he shoved the tip into the hull. Biceps straining, he pushed down, forcing the sword through the black metal. Time seemed to stand still as Taurian produced a makeshift door. In mere seconds, he was shoving through leading his band of screaming thugs into battle. When a warm body jostled Adelaide, she jerked forward, following Cullen onto the enemy ship. She had to inspect Taurian's sword when the battle was won. How the hell did it do that? Was the colour significant?

With snarls, they spread out, searching the cargo bay for the enemy. Cullen stuck close to her as they stepped behind a large crate, their weapons held aloft. She squinted her eyes, trying to discern any movement in the dark shadows.

"How can anyone see?" Cullen grumbled.

"The Tu'Val have superior vision. I'm sure they're having no issues." She pushed a few buttons on her comm. A faint glow emitted, nudging back the shadows.

A loud hiss sounded, echoing across the large room.

"Masks!" Taurian yelled. "To the door."

Adelaide grabbed at her waist, yanking the mask as she ran towards the other warriors. When she placed it against her face, it shifted, molding to cover her eyes, mouth and nose. Gasping in surprise, she glanced around for Cullen, who was right behind her. "We need these." She pointed to her face.

"Move over," Taurian ordered, facing the exit with his glowing sword. He jumped to the side as the formed door fell away, followed by blaster fire.

Adelaide ducked rolling towards Taurian. She spotted four black shaped creatures out the corner of her eye.

"Do you have a bomb?" Adelaide yelled at Taurian.

He glanced over with a huge grin, holding a small tubular object. He wound his arm, releasing the object through the top corner of the doorway. Seconds later, smoke billowed through the entryway. Adelaide covered her ears as multiple shrieks sounded.

Where was the boom? she wondered. There was supposed to be a boom. Why weren't the Tu'Val covering their ears?

"Go! Go!" Taurian yelled charging forward.

They converged into the dimly lit hallway. Taurian and a couple of his men battled the one Cradesion still standing while the other warriors trampled over the three black bodies, splitting in opposite directions down the hallway.

"I say we stick with Taurian," Cullen said as Taurian swiped the Cradesion with his sword. Black blood oozed out of the severed neck while its body fell. The head rolled to their feet.

"I don't think so. Taurian will probably hold us back. Let's go." Grinning, she turned to the right at a run. Cullen swore, but his steps followed behind. Lights blinked in the corridor. Distant screams and yells came from the right.

A door slid open, a Raykar stepping out, his hand gripping a large sword.

Adelaide barreled full steam ahead, taking the Raykar to the ground.

"Fucking what the hell?" Cullen yelled stopping besides, aiming for the enemy.

In one fluid move, Adelaide swiped downward with her knife, using her momentum to penetrate the Raykar's eye and deeper, into its brain. Adelaide jumped back, wiping her blade across her thigh, and turned to Cullen.

His mouth hung open a moment before he cleared his throat. "You just—"

"Move it, man—more to kill, more to discover. Maybe we'll find the rest of the survivors from Tikaani." Adelaide nudged him, knife in one hand, a laser in the other. Green blood slid down her chest, splattering on the black metal wall as she spun running forward.

As his footsteps thudded behind her, adrenalin flooded Adelaide's body. She missed this; delivering cargo didn't have this much action.

She couldn't help but chuckle, picturing Cullen's face. Had he thought she was some wilting flower? Heading down the corridor, she checked for the medical room. Their tech was years ahead; she'd probably have to hide it from Taurian. An open door beckoned, she slowly entered. Jackpot.

"Hurry up, Cullen," she hissed, rushing to the drawers.

"What are we searching for?" Cullen followed her lead, flinging open cupboards.

"Any unusual tech you can fit on your person. Hurry before we're caught."

Muted sounds of combat filtered into the room, the volume increasing as the door slid open, revealing two Raykar. Cullen spun, firing as he dove to the left. Though his shot hit one in the stomach, the Raykar barely flinched.

"Fuck!" Cullen yelled as both he and Adelaide ran at the enemy.

Adelaide began trading blows, swinging her sword to incapacitate the enemy in front of her. Cullen pulled out a knife, ducking and weaving to avoid being stabbed. He stumbled over a box just as the Raykar bellowed a war cry, advancing at an unbelievable speed. Cullen pivoted, thrusting his knife while simultaneously firing his laser. Jabbing all the way to the hilt Cullen grunted as the Raykar's sword sliced a long cut along his arm, from shoulder to elbow. He fired again opening a hole through the Raykar's stomach, the body collapsed. Cullen clutched his arm as he surveyed the room.

"Fuck, this is exciting." Adelaide grinned, wiping her sword on the body. "Are you alright? You're leaking on the floor."

"I'm fine. We're in a med bay. I should be able to find something to bandage my arm temporarily."

"Let's finish searching and get out of here." Adelaide continued rifling through the shelving and cupboards while Cullen wrapped a bandage around his arm.

A few minutes later, Adelaide yelled, "Bingo!" holding up a thin tube about three inches in length with a spinning blue point at the end. "Let's go." She stuffed it along with the few other items into her pocket.

Leaving the room, Adelaide led the way, heading directly towards the fighting. Cullen stalked beside her, fingering his laser. He muttered, words indistinguishable.

She glanced over. "Have something to say?"

"Just a prayer."

Startled, she said, "You believe?"

"Not really, but it couldn't hurt, following you around."

Laughing, Adelaide pulled ahead.

The ship lurched, and the haze of smoke grew thicker. Rubbing her eyes, Adelaide planted her feet. She tried waving the smoke away while peering ahead at the bodies littering the corridor. What seemed to be two Raykar, a Cradesion and a Tu'Val—sounded like the start of a bad joke—were engaged ahead.

Motioning to Cullen, Adelaide surged forward, weaving between the still forms on the floor Cullen fired, removing the Raykar threat allowing the Tu'Val to finish off the Cradesion. They entered another room, finding Taurian battling a Cradesion in full armour. A Raykar ran from the right, sword held aloft, straight for Taurian's back. Not on her watch, bastard.

She fired, leaving a red, glowing hole through his head. The body dropped. Taurian destroyed his opponent before glancing back.

"I knew you cared." He grinned before sprinting in the opposite direction. Blood dripped down his back from multiple cuts as he disappeared from view.

"Let's go, Cullen. We need to find the brig."

"If it is the same schematics as the ship we were on, the cells should be this way." Cullen took the lead.

Battle sounds echoed around them. Adelaide stepped gingerly past a pile of guts lying beside a headless Raykar body. Her nose wrinkled from the odor. Did they not bathe?

"Where in the hell is the rest of it?" Cullen whispered.

"Don't think about it."

He nodded and picked up the pace. They didn't want to be left behind.

The farther they strode, the quieter it became. So the sound of screams and laser fire startled her into jumping.

"Come on," she yelled running full out.

When they rounded the corner, she spotted a Cradesion raising its weapon to fire on a prisoner cowering in the cell. His body was littered with cuts, his dark blue shirt hanging on by a few strips of fabric across his shoulders. Other prisoners were yelling for help, but more lay silently, never to rise again.

"Fucker!" Adelaide screamed firing her laser while pulling out her sword. Cullen was right behind her.

The Cradesion returned fire, and they dove to the ground with Adelaide rolling back up swinging. One of the creature's arms fell, followed by an ear-piercing shriek. She kept attacking, a maniacal grin across her face. The bastard was so cock sure no one could hurt it while killing unarmed people. With only one laser they were soon able to destroy him. Breathing heavily, Adelaide bent over, her hands braced against her knees as she took stock of her injuries. It was better than she hoped. Her arm began to ache—a delayed reaction from a laser burn.

"You alive Cullen?"

"Yes. You're crazy lady." He shook his head, moving toward the cells. "We need to find the control room to unlock these. Unless he had a key."

Adelaide rummaged around the body before holding up a key in triumph. "Let's blow this Popsicle stand." Sadness washed over Adelaide as she faced the surviving prisoners. "I'm sorry we couldn't get here any sooner."

The ship shook, groaning and screeching as if it were about to crumble. Time to go.

"Red, where are you?" Taurian demanded over the comm.

"We found the survivors. On our way."

"Move it, Red. You don't want me to come and find you."

Adelaide muttered under her breath as they helped the ten remaining prisoners move.

"You were at the cave," one woman stated.

"Yes." Adelaide glanced over. The woman looked to be in her early twenties, long, straggly black hair, blue eyes. It took everything in Adelaide not to cringe when she helped the girl walk. First thing was the doctor, then a shower.

"Move it, Adelaide!" Cullen yelled, as he turned the corner a cloud of smoke enveloped his form. Sirens blared, and Adelaide ducked as a section of the ceiling collapsed, sending sparks in their direction.

"I know you're in pain, but we have to run," Adelaide said.

The girl grunted before picking up her speed. A few Tu'Val ran towards them, grabbing the survivors and slinging them over their shoulders before taking off despite their weak objections.

"Adelaide, you still on board the Cradesion ship?" Gil's voice came over her comm.

"Yeah, we're on our way out. What's going on?"

"Get out now! There's been a surge in their engines. I think it's going to blow."

Adelaide stumbled as the ship went dark. *Damn it.* Emergency lights activated, casting a faint glow that she could continue to follow.

"Move it everyone the ship is going to blow!"

Not even bothering to avoid the blood and guts littering the floors any longer they ran into the cargo bay where Taurian was waiting.

"Red, you made it. Any slower and I might have had to come rescue you."

"You wish," Adelaide said breathlessly. "Move it, Gil said there was a surge in the engines."

Minutes after Taurian's ship disengaged there was a loud explosion, the ship spun slightly.

Adelaide felt like collapsing. She let the wall hold her up as she calmed her heartrate.

"You alright?" Cullen asked looking how Adelaide felt.

"Yeah, give me a minute." Adelaide moved carefully over to examine the cargo bay and the remaining crew. She didn't know how many had headed over, but it didn't appear like they had lost many. Some who had severe wounds were being carried out towards the med bay. "Gil, we made it."

"Alright, hand them over." Taurian stalked over to them, pointing at the cabinets.

"Sure, no problem," Cullen said.

They both placed their weapons back into their original locations.

"And the others," Taurian said, eyebrows wiggling.

"That was all of it," Adelaide said.

"Do you want to be searched? I'm more than willing to check your body for anything." He was so smug, she wanted to punch him.

"I hate you," she hissed, yanking the items out of her pockets, nodding at Cullen to do the same.

"We've already established you don't." Taurian laughed, grabbing the items, handing them off to one of his men. "Anything else?"

"No." She scowled, standing straight even though her body wanted to drop. "Are we done here?"

"Yes. Head to the doctor first. Then we will debrief. Meet you on the bridge. You both fought well tonight." Taurian turned, disappearing among the others.

Adelaide gawked at Cullen in surprise.

"Praise? How shocking," Cullen said as they headed to the med bay, holding each other up.

"Let's get your arm stitched up," Adelaide said.

Stumbling into each other, they received nods from the crew. At least they proved their worth, and hopefully Taurian would be willing to share more. The door slid open. Adelaide stood straighter as she searched for a place to collapse and wait her turn. The doctor was working on the prisoners. It didn't look like he would get to them anytime soon.

"Come on, Cullen. Let's find some first aid. We can at least get most of our wounds doctored ourselves."

He nodded, following as she weaved between the patients to the back cabinet.

"Hey, Doc. I'm grabbing some supplies," Adelaide called as she searched through the cabinet.

Chapter 10

Adelaide shifted from foot to foot, watching as Gil guided the Clandestine into the cargo bay of Taurian's ship. It seemed to take forever as the ship stopped, slowly powering down.

"What do you think happened that Gil isn't telling us?" Cullen asked, inspecting their ship for any damage.

"I'm not sure, but I'll get answers."

The instant she spotted Gil as the doors opened, Adelaide ran forward onto the Clandestine's ramp, enveloping Gil with shaking arms. Damn protocol.

Gil patted her back. "Glad to see you, kiddo." His voice was gruff.

She nodded her head into his neck, slowly releasing him.

"What the hell is wrong with you?" She smacked his arm, stepping away with a frown.

"I've had enough of those idiots; that's why I left the military the first time." Gil smirked before walking around her towards Cullen.

"Glad you made it out. Sorry about Bastion." He shook Cullen's hand.

"Thanks, man. Glad to be here. Not sure how sane this place is though." Cullen glanced in Adelaide's direction, then away.

Gil laughed following Cullen's eyes. "Could have told you as much."

With Adelaide, they headed to meet Taurian at the other side of the cargo bay for Bastion's send off. The original plan was to take Bastion to his home, but they didn't have time. This could be done now for him, his family had agreed.

The doctor had wrapped Bastion's body in cloth, then laid him on a floating gurney. Taurian solemnly watched their approach, then turned facing the window.

Adelaide glanced at Cullen. "Do you want to say anything?"

"Alright." He proceeded to say a few words highlighting their times together.

Adelaide stared at the body, her mind wandering back to their cage and the last time she'd seen him alive. He had gone out fighting, not taking any shit from their captors. Sniffling, she watched as Taurian pressed his comm. The chute opened, pulling Bastion firing him into space. Taurian lightly placed his hand on her shoulder for a moment before leaving them alone.

"I hope he's at peace." She sighed, knowing more comrades would fall during the upcoming battles.

"So what's the plan?" Gil asked.

"I'm waiting for revised orders." She pulled a face. "I demanded the general confer with the Syndicate. Earth wants nothing to do with the Tu'Val."

"Idiots." Cullen turned from watching Bastion's body float away.

"And the general wanted me to inform you of impending disciplinary action."

Gil grinned. "Sure. I'll keep that in mind."

Adelaide shook her head. "Gil, you need to be cautious. I don't want to see you in the blockades."

"Won't happen. I'm sure Taurian will allow me asylum. Especially if I promise you'll come along."

Cullen laughed as they left the bay.

Adelaide growled, pushing down the butterflies. "I don't think so. Where are your friends?"

"They determined staying aboard the Clandestine would be prudent."

"Probably a good idea." Adelaide nodded. "Taurian doesn't like outsiders on his ship. He's tolerating Cullen right now."

Gil glanced at Adelaide before turning away. "I may also have one military personnel on board."

Stopping, Adelaide glared at Gil, her hands on her hips. "What the hell, Gil!"

He winced. "It wasn't in the plan."

"Doesn't matter, Gil. You've now guaranteed his military future is over and put us all at risk," she hissed, looking around the room for listeners.

Gil straightened. "Hey, I didn't kidnap him. Edward refused to leave—he strongly disagreed with certain orders. The general may not know about him yet.

He's in engineering, not an officer." Gil lowered his voice. "There are situations you need to be aware of."

"Fine, let's head back to the Clandestine, and you can explain this shit show. But we have to hurry. Taurian wants a meeting." She turned and stomped towards the ship with Gil and Cullen trailing behind.

Once they entered, Adelaide slapped her hand on the controls, closing the doors. "Spill it," she demanded of Gil.

"When the survivors were beamed aboard, the med bot scanned them, searching for injuries. In twenty of them, it discovered"—he cleared his throat—"*eggs*."

Adelaide looked at him in horror.

"No, you can't mean what I'm thinking?" Cullen said.

Gil nodded. "Yes, we put them in stasis hoping it slows the growth. Earth wanted to allow the eggs to come to term in order to study the creatures." He ran his hand down his face, sighing.

"What the fuck!" Adelaide yelled, pacing. "I can't believe the general would condone this."

"He did. Said it was for the good of Earth."

"We can't let them do that. Can't the eggs be removed?" Cullen asked.

"They didn't want to try."

"So, you have them on board here?" Adelaide asked.

"Yes. We're hoping to find a way to have them safely removed or, if necessary, destroyed."

"As in killing the host? What kind of option is that?" Cullen demanded, glaring at Gil.

"Would you want those things in you? Or what if they do hatch? We don't know what will happen, how strong they will be. Would they kill everyone before they could be slaughtered?"

Cullen grimaced.

"How did you plan on finding out?" Adelaide asked.

Gil collapsed on a nearby container. "I was hoping we could test the waters with Taurian, hypothetically to see if his government would do the right thing. Their honor is everything to them so hopefully this would fall into their 'want to help' area. If the eggs can be removed safely, they could be studied in a controlled environment with plenty of shielding without hurting anyone else."

"Okay, here is what we will do." Adelaide stopped pacing staring at the other two. "Not a word about this to anyone."

"No one else knows accept Edward because he helped hide the survivors."

"I will feel out Taurian and decide if we can ask for his help. Otherwise, we need to find a different solution for removing the eggs. Gil, you oversee monitoring the eggs' growth and informing me of the progress. If you need to involve Edward, fine. But he better be sworn to secrecy or it's his head. Understood?" She growled out the words.

"Yes, Captain," they both responded.

"Let's get to Taurian's bridge before he's too suspicious and starts asking questions I'm not ready to answer." Adelaide opened the door and headed back into the cargo bay.

They stepped around a warrior standing at attention entering the bridge.

"Commander, thank you for the assistance with Bastion," Adelaide said.

Taurian dipped his head. "Honouring the dead is essential. Are there any problems?"

"No, Gil was just updating me on the statis of our mission."

"Commander," the ensign called, "there is a hail from General Tahoun."

"Put it through." Taurian leaned forward, eyes focused on the screen.

"Commander."

"What have you discovered?"

"The location of a small enemy force."

"What are the coordinates and movements?"

"They've just released two shuttles, which are heading to the planet."

"Hold position. We will rendezvous."

The screen went blank.

"Do you want to send us the coordinates and we'll meet you there?" Adelaide asked.

"Don't worry; your ship can stay docked with us so you won't get lost." Taurian's lips quirked. "Show our new guests' quarters they can stay in," he said to the warrior standing beside them.

Gil glanced over. "No problem, Taurian. We can stay on the Clandestine."

The crew tensed, glaring in Gil's direction. Probably for being on a first name basis with their commander.

"That might be for the best."

"Ju djaizf nu om yju ntohh," the ensign said.

"Umaihj, yjup etu ait ezzoud ey yjod yoqu," Taurian replied.

"What did he say?" Cullen whispered.

"You don't want to know," she responded from the corner of her mouth.

"Commander, we have the coordinates."

"Plot a course. What is the expected arrival time?"

There was silence for a moment. "We will arrive late tomorrow."

"Engage. Inform High Command we will need additional ships." Taurian swivelled his attention to Gil and Adelaide. "I think a tour of the Clandestine would be a great idea." He stood, eyeing them expectantly.

Gil turned to Adelaide with a frown. It was one thing running from their military it was another letting a non-ally on board. But what choice did they have? the Tu'Val warriors could take them out and have complete access. At least with them in charge, they may be able to keep their portable gate hidden.

"Sure, Commander. This way." Adelaide turned sideways to wave him past.

Gil regarded her for a moment before following. Taurian and two warriors led the way to the Clandestine.

"Taurian, we will show you the ship, but we won't allow your warriors," Adelaide said as the ship came into sight.

The two in question grunted. "Humutez yjod odm may stavaz."

"I will be fine," Taurian said. "You think a few puny humans can contain me in my own ship?" With a snarl, he took a step towards his men.

"No, Commander."

"Leave. We will not be long."

The two warriors stepped back, their hands hovering over their lasers. Taurian growled, they moved farther away, dropping their hands, standing stiff at attention.

"This is a magnificent ship." He ran his hand along the hull, walking towards the ramp.

Adelaide grinned. "It is amazing." She stepped onto the ramp heading into the cargo bay, the men behind her. She strode through the ship at a quick pace, hoping Taurian wouldn't notice every little detail.

"We'll head to the bridge now." She turned to lead the way.

Taurian had been silent up to this point. "What about engineering?"

"That isn't on the tour." Crossing her arms, Adelaide stopped, waiting for his objections.

"I could make you," he said quietly, stepping closer to her.

When Cullen placed his hand over his laser, she subtly shook her head.

"Maybe, but do you really want to? Gil is here on his own accord; you didn't capture the ship. You don't want us to come to blows."

Taurian flashed his teeth at Cullen. "I would not make rash decisions to threaten me. Red may hold some regard to me, but you have not achieved that status."

He addressed Adelaide with a slight nod. "I will hold off at this time. In the future, it could change."

"We'll see." She spun, stomping down the corridor. "Until the access to your engineering room is opened, ours will remain closed."

Taurian chuckled behind her, and she shook her head, loosening her muscles.

When the door to the bridge slid open, Adelaide beamed. It almost felt like home.

"Hello, Adelaide. How are you, girl?" An older gentleman approached her, his blue eyes twinkling. As she was enfolded in a large embrace, Taurian grumbled behind her.

Speaking against his chest, she said, "Albert, it's great to see you. I should have guessed Gil would rope you into this. Are the others here?"

Albert released her, stepping away so she could see the four other men all watching silently.

Gil's old troop back together again. She prayed no one got in their way. They have been one of the top infiltrating teams in the military with minimum casualties.

"What the hell, Adelaide? We came for a fight, and we're hung out to dry." A small, green male sighed.

"Maybe you should be recaptured so we can have some fun."

"I'll get right on it, Bato. Should I also be crying in the corner waiting for rescue?" She laughed.

"That would be considerate."

"Who are these males?" Taurian marched into Adelaide's personal space, glaring around the room.

"No offense to them, but they're too old for me." Adelaide tried to push him away.

"Why would you not want these male specimens? They are all in their prime."

"Oh, for the love of Pete." Her cheeks pinkened as the others laughed. "Humans don't usually date with a big age difference."

When Gil snorted, she shot a glare his direction.

"Why not?" Taurian demanded. "They have the experience and wisdom."

"Yeah, Adelaide. Why not?" Albert chuckled.

"Ew, not happening. Just drop it, Taurian."

Probably feeling pity for her, Gil walked farther onto the bridge. "They're from my old squad."

Taurian peered at him in surprise. "They are not all human." He gestured forward.

Adelaide bit her tongue from saying "No shit, Sherlock." He probably wouldn't get the reference anyway, and she'd have to explain.

"Later in the war, Earth banded with others from the Accords, finding the diversity worked well."

Taurian rubbed his chin. "I am surprised Earth was so strategic. During our dealings with them, they only wanted humans on their teams." He sneered.

"Anyhoo," Adelaide said, finally pushing Taurian's massive body so she could move. "What is the plan?"

"We will rendezvous with my ships."

"Commander, High Command is on comms."

"I will take the message in the ready room." Taurian nodded in their direction before striding off the bridge.

Adelaide and Gil eyeballed each other. She dipped her head, then waved to the others before running out with Cullen behind her. She wasn't letting Taurian out of her sight.

Behind her, Gil said, "It's time, men."

"Taurian, wait!" Her legs might be a decent length, but they had to work double time to match his stride.

He glanced back, expression smug. "You need to keep up, Red, or you will miss the action." His pace slowed slightly as she came abreast, walking at his side until they reached the bridge and headed into the ready room.

Taurian sat, pushing a button on the table. The screen in front wavered before a large Tu'Val male face appeared.

"Commander. Based on the data, we will send additional ships to the supplied coordinates."

"How many ships?"

"Three war ships are currently en route."

"I will keep you informed of our progress."

The screen went blank. Taurian pushed another button. "Inform me when we are at our destination. I will be in my quarters." He rose, grabbed Adelaide's arm, and dragged her behind him onto the bridge. Cullen growled, but the noise stopped when some of the crew stepped closer.

"I can walk myself," she hissed, tugging at her arm.

"I know. We should make the most of our time in case the enemy triumphs. Cullen can head to his own quarters."

She stopped in shock, stumbling as he pulled.

"Adelaide?" Cullen asked, pushing forward.

"It's fine. I'll see you later." She watched as Cullen left before turning to Taurian. "I . . . I don't think so. Damn it, let go." Her cheeks warmed, her heart beating faster.

Taurian grinned, wiggling his brows. "You are sure? I sensed hesitation there. Maybe you need an incentive."

When he tugged this time, she fell against his hard, sculpted body. His lips took her thoughts away. It was minutes before she could coherently pull back, breathing heavily.

"I'll take a rain check."

Taurian regarded her, confusion in his eyes. At least she wasn't the only one affected—his chest rose and fell rapidly as well.

"Later." Adelaide strode quickly back to her room, berating herself for getting involved. Her back twitched; she felt Taurian's eyes following her.

Ensuring her door was sealed, Adelaide sent an encrypted message to the general. With no coordinates,

she could only let command know about the Cradesion
fleet and await her orders.

Chapter 11

Beeping woke Adelaide from a deep sleep. She swiped her hand across her tired, grubby eyes. Slowly sitting up, she slid her legs over the bedside. The loud, annoying sound continued while she checked who was contacting her. Her lips turned down.

"General, you received my report?"

"Yes, Captain."

"What are my orders?"

"You're to stand down. Observe only."

Adelaide regarded him in shock. "Didn't you see they're going into battle? They could use our weaponry."

The general scowled. "Watch it, Captain. I'm your superior."

"Sorry, sir. I can't just stand by while they get destroyed."

"Those are your orders, Captain, and that is Earth's ship."

Adelaide clenched her fists, trying to keep her face blank. "Yes sir. May I ask the reason?"

"The Tu'Val aren't our allies. You will observe and send back intel on our enemy. Do you understand?"

She nodded. "Yes sir. What if the Tu'Val are slaughtered?"

"You have a ship; use it to escape." Her comm went black.

Adelaide swore, standing and stomping around the bed. "What the fuck is wrong with those idiots? I'm not just standing around."

A knock interrupted her.

Spinning, Adelaide faced the door. "What?" she barked.

The door slid open. "What crawled up your ass?" Cullen asked, grinning, "Didn't your date with Taurian go well?"

She grimaced. "Let's go for a walk."

They headed to the Clandestine's bridge, Cullen striding beside her.

"We have a problem," she said when they arrived.

Six sets of eyes stared in silence.

She took a deep breath. "Our orders are to do nothing."

"What the fuck?" Cullen said as Gil swore. The others laughed.

"We don't have to listen," Connor said with a grin. He had been with Gil the longest. Connor loved to fight, and he had the look. Standing at six foot four with broad shoulders and inked arms, he was no wilting flower. Adelaide knew he had helped Gil get out of a few scrapes. No one messed with Connor's friends.

"What are we doing, Captain?" Gil asked. "You know what my opinion would be."

Her lips curled. Yeah, she knew what he thought of the military.

"I will not stand aside and watch the Tu'Val battle an enemy we should all be fighting; I don't agree with Earth's order." Adelaide paced. "I know sometimes a soldier won't agree with an order from command, but you still need to follow. This order could be a detriment to Earth. It's very short sighted." She sighed collapsing in her chair. Her stomach hurt; she didn't like going against her commander.

"Will we fly the Clandestine?" Gil asked.

"Let's wait and see. Maybe they can use us elsewhere and we won't be completely disregarding orders."

"We'll await your command," Bato said.

"Adelaide, where are you?" Taurian's voice filled the room.

"I'm on the Clandestine."

"We will be arriving at the coordinates shortly."

"We'll be right there." She signed off and faced the others. "No one mention Earth's stand in this skirmish. Let's go, Cullen."

* * *

"Move it." A warrior pushed past them in the corridor. A few more followed him, grins plastered on their faces. Adelaide always felt the adrenalin rush before a battle, but they took it too the extreme. They found Taurian in his element, growling orders while lounging in the captain's chair.

"Have the other ships arrived?" he demanded, staring at the ensign.

"They are minutes away." The ensign swiped his finger across the screen.

"Send this message to our fleet."

Taurian stood, hands on his hips, body covered in weapons. He came across as strong and threatening. Adelaide wouldn't want to meet him in the dark.

As Taurian gave his orders, awe filled the younger crew members' faces, while resolve showed in the others. His speech was inspirational. Ten warships moved into formation on the screen, advanced as one unit. The scouts had reported no change to the Cradesion fleet. About fifty smaller black ships came into view. A chill ran up Adelaide's spine as the newcomers attacked the Tu'Val warships. Taurian shouted orders as his ship tilted. Adelaide rolled with turbulence, loosening her muscles to maintain her balance. The floor shuddered as shots made contact; Taurian's ship returned fire.

"Evasive manoeuvres!"

A bright light burst on the screen. Shrapnel flew in front as a Cradesion ship blew apart. Adelaide grinned; they weren't so bad.

"Commander, two of their smaller ships are splitting off and heading to the planet surface."

Taurian sneered at the escaping vessels.

"Are they meeting the shuttles they sent earlier? We will take two shuttles and pursue. Contact the fleet with an update."

"Yes sir."

"Commander, do you want the Clandestine to join?" Adelaide knew the guys would be getting antsy.

"We will keep it in reserve; we do not need them."

Adelaide shrugged; she'd offered.

Taurian barked orders into his comm unit on the way to the shuttle bay.

"Commander." A warrior stepped away from the wall, intercepting their group. "Who do you want with you?"

"We need crews for two shuttles; ensure the doctor is there."

"Yes, Commander." He saluted then shifted so Taurian could stomp past. Adelaide and Cullen scurried after; she wasn't sure if Taurian even remembered they were there.

Without looking back, Taurian said, "Contact Gil. Inform him he is accompanying us."

"You can't order me to supply men." Adelaide frowned at Taurian's golden hair. *Turn around, damn it.*

"I am the commander. This is my ship upon which your crew are guests. You want to participate?" He turned his head, lips quirked. "Then you follow my orders."

Adelaide swore under her breath though Cullen nudged her from behind, whispering, "Yes."

"Fine. I will follow your orders, but not blindly. I'm with Earth's military." She pressed her comm unit. "Gil, we're going on an adventure. Get your ass weaponized, then meet us in the shuttle bay. You have a few minutes."

"Yes, Captain." Glee filled his voice.

The urge to either punch Taurian or stick her tongue out at him came over her as he chuckled.

"We'll meet you after grabbing some supplies, Commander." Adelaide clenched her teeth as she pushed past, heading to the Clandestine.

She nodded to a grinning Gil as they passed each other on the Clandestine's cargo plank.

In her quarters, Adelaide pulled on black pants, a fitted black T-shirt and her boots. After strapping on her knives and laser guns, she slipped into her rescued jacket.

Smiling, she patted the chest; the scientists would have killed her for losing it, not that they were getting it back. Striding out of the Clandestine, she headed for the grey shuttles, which looked like every other shuttle she'd ever seen. The hatch opened at the rear. Engine cells, used as stabilizers, ran the length of the shuttle on either side.

Taurian watched as she drew closer, his possessive gaze travelling the length of her body.

"Are we ready to go?" Cullen asked, bouncing on the balls of his feet.

Taurian directed everyone to the shuttles, ensuring Adelaide's crew remained with him along with a couple of his warriors. Sitting in the pilot's seat, he pushed a few buttons. Adelaide sat in one of the eight chairs in the back, wanting to be closest to the exit. Taurian was piloting, and she didn't know how competent he was.

"We need to hurry; they separated after entering the planet's atmosphere," Taurian growled, as the shuttle flew into space.

The shuttle hull groaned. Something clanged as they weaved around the debris and fighting ships. Adelaide's heartrate increased. As the battle played out through her window, she clenched the arm rests. It was completely different being a passenger on a piddly ship compared to captaining a starship. Cullen groaned in front of her as Taurian spun the shuttle, skimming past a large piece of metal.

She laughed quietly, wanting to yell out "Wheee!" They descended, following the trail through the white-and-red clouds. Adelaide shifted in her seat, watching the others in the cockpit.

The doctor smiled at her. "You have a question?"

She tilted her head. "Yeah, no offense, but why didn't you stay on the ship? Won't they need you more because of the battle?"

"I go where the commander does." He spread his hands, falling silent.

"Okay." Adelaide drew out the word. His response wasn't an answer.

"Should we destroy the ship?" the warrior in front inquired.

"Have they landed?" Taurian demanded keeping focused on his screen.

"Yes sir. The system detects four lifeforms, moving away."

"Any life signs on the ship?"

"Our sensors cannot penetrate the hull."

"Fire until it is disabled; it will give us the chance to inspect the ship."

"This shuttle can disable a ship?" Adelaide asked.

Taurian raised an eyebrow. "Of course, Are Earth's not as advanced?"

Adelaide muttered under her breath while Taurian chuckled. Earth's shuttles didn't have anything like that kind of fire power; she wasn't even sure if their shields could hold up. The seats vibrated as they fired on the enemy shuttle. *Ha, not smooth.*

"Commander, the ship is disabled."

"We will land close and disembark. Inform the other shuttle of our location, I want a status update." Taurian's left hand was steady on the yoke as his right flew over the controls.

After a soft thud and bump, the hatch opened, letting a cool breeze blow through the shuttle.

"Spread out, watch for any threats. Sensors show they headed towards those mountains." Taurian indicated the direction. "We will follow them first to disable, then inspect their ship."

Large blue rocks peeked over the horizon. Adelaide gazed in wonder at the waist-high blue-green grass. A few steps off the ramp, she ran her hand along the tops, surprised by the soft tickle on the bottom of her hand. Narrowing her eyes, she surveyed the area, expecting something to jump out from the as-far-as-she-could-see prairie. Leaving the doctor to man the shuttle, the rest of them walked for about five minutes, when a loud caw sounded in the distance, growing shriller.

"What's that?" Gil asked, squinting into the blue sky.

They all watched as the black speck increased in size.

"Drop!" Adelaide screamed.

Three huge creatures dived at them, emitting nail-against-slate screeches. Gigantic talons stretched, raking for victims. The black feathers along their legs emphasized their red, featherless bodies. Adelaide lay in a defensive position, arms covering her head. A scream, this one human, tore through the air. She glanced from under her arm. One of Taurian's warriors was clutched by his shoulders, while the beast's black wings flapped. The span was large enough to kick up wind, making the grasses swish in a frenzy. The creature quickly ascended to the sky.

"Givl," Taurian yelled, standing. He fired his laser. His aim was true, but the laser bounced off its body.

"Try for it's head," she suggested as they all joined in.

One of their shots exploded on target, causing both man and beast to plummet to the ground. The soldier, pinned underneath the carcass, lay still as the creature's friends screeched and flew away. Taurian rolled the body over.

"Shavel, are you alive?" he demanded.

Shavel groaned, his body shifting slightly.

Taurian barked orders into his comm as he stooped down, inspecting Shavel. His right leg was bent at the wrong angle.

In minutes, the doctor ran towards them, pushing a floating gurney. Shavel screamed as he was lifted.

"This should help." The doctor placed a med strip onto Shavel's arm.

Adelaide sighed as silence reigned.

"Doctor, can you repair him in the shuttle?" Taurian asked.

"I may be able to stabilize him until we can rejoin with the ship. I will need help setting his leg." The doctor hovered over Shavel, his hands lightly inspecting his body.

"Creden, you go to the shuttle with the doctor. When Shavel is stable, follow our trail." Taurian paced, grumbling until the three crewmen disappeared into the shuttle. Then, he said, "Let's move."

They set off at a brisk pace, spreading apart, weapons out and on alert.

Adelaide sniffed, trying to place the woodsy, pungent smell. Lifting her hand to shade her eyes, she asked, "How much farther?"

"Their ship is right over this rise," Taurian said. "The Cradesions are now stationary, not too far from their ship. One life sign has disappeared."

The tall grass whipping against them as they moved through. Smoke rose in the distance; the cause became apparent as they crested the hill. A black-blue ship crushed the tall grass, a small hole in the hull could be seen from their location.

"At least it's still intact," Gil stated.

"Commander," a voice said over the comm.

"Report."

"We lost three ships, destroyed half the Cradesion's fleet the rest are fleeing. Do we pursue?"

"Good news. No, I want the rest of our ships to stay in orbit until we determine what they are doing here. Have one of the scout ships tail behind the fleeing enemy and send us intelligence." Shoulders tense, Taurian strode on with jerky steps.

Adelaide wondered how many soldiers he had lost. She hurried to Taurian's side. "I'm sorry for the loss of your men."

Taurian glanced over. "Thank you. They are at peace and fought well for their people. We will remember their sacrifice."

To the left, a forest with brown and black trees came into view. Right in front stood their destination of rocks.

Adelaide glanced behind at the swath they made through the grass. No way their path couldn't be spotted. She sighed. "How the hell did they make it this far without leaving a trail?"

Cullen gazed over. "Good question." His body twitched as a roar came from the trees. "Could they have boosters, making it possible to fly over?"

Taurian lifted a hand, halting at the abrupt edge of the tall grass. The next step would be onto a brown, earthen crust with numerous blue and red rock formations. Sporadic tuffs of green foliage dotted the surface. A burble emanated somewhere to their left closer to the forest, a place Adelaide could almost guarantee she didn't want to go.

"To our right are the three lifeforms. Keep watch for another creature," Taurian whispered.

"Along with all the native creatures," Cullen muttered.

Adelaide smirked. "Come on, Cullen. You wanted excitement and adventure."

"That was Gil, over there." Cullen gestured while Gil chuckled, following close behind Taurian.

A rustling sounded from behind, and they all whipped around.

"Commander?" Creden whispered.

"Damn it. Don't scare me You're lucky I didn't shoot." Cullen frowned, lowering his laser.

"Did you detect anyone?" Taurian asked.

"No sir."

Taurian cautiously stepped onto the crushed rocks, dust rising into the air.

"Givl!" Taurian yelled, dropping to the ground. The rest of them followed.

"What the hell, Taurian?" Adelaide called, hearing a hum.

"Someone is shooting."

Great, Adelaide thought, *and no cover.*

Searching the area, she tried to spot the shooter. A light came from the left, then another hum.

"Move, move!" she screamed scrambling to the right while firing towards the source.

"Fuck!" Cullen yelled, as a hole opened in the ground by his body.

They all open fired, hoping someone would make contact. The trees exploded, spitting wood shrapnel in every direction. Sharp wood chips bounce off her coat sleeves. Swearing filled the area, some of them weren't so lucky. A screech emitted from the forest, then silence.

"Cover me," Adelaide whispered to Gil's prone body beside her. He nodded, and at a crouch, she weaved through the grass. Faltering as her leg cramped, she paused to study the trees. A laser burned just meters away from her head. Swearing, she scuttled sideways then ran full tilt towards the source.

"Go, go!" Gil yelled from behind. His laser flew past her, exploding a small tree. Panting, Adelaide skidded to a halt just inside the forest, behind a large black tree. A crunch sounded under her feet. Damn it, those looked like bones. Swiping at the green oval leaves, Adelaide stepped farther into the dark. Small lights flickered to the left; a loud roar followed by a screech came from the right. Go towards the pretty lights or the terrible noises? Such a difficult choice.

She smirked before skirting around the tree trunk. Her hand hovered over the purple moss covering the trunk. What was that stuff? Her nose wrinkled as a sour smell reached her. Sniffing again, Adelaide jerked her hand away, moving quickly towards the excitement. She twitched whenever a bone crunched, echoing between the trees. At a massive brown trunk towering above the surrounding plants, she stopped, spreading her arms in wonder, as they only reached half the width of the spectacular specimen. It was also covered by the unknown purple substance. Peering closer, Adelaide spotted tiny creatures moving in and out of the moss. Their bodies were no larger than her pinky nail but the pinchers on their front legs were massive, about double the size of their bodies. *How could they move so easily without toppling over?* Their little red bodies scurried around the trunk, some carrying items clenched in their pinchers.

Growls ahead jerked Adelaide's attention. She bolted forward, stopping before a clearing just as a crash of trees sounded. She stared in amazement. A Cradesion battled against a blue, furry body. There were no weapons in sight. The Cradesion's four arms struggled to hold the large body at bay.

Its back claws dug into the Cradesion's leg armor as the pair screeched and growled at each other. She might as well let them go at it. Hopefully, the creature would win. Lifting her gun, she spun around, monitoring the rustling of leaves.

Gil stepped out. "You're alive." He crouched beside her.

She grinned. "Of course." Gesturing towards the battle, she said, "I'm waiting for the winner. How did you find me?"

"I followed the screams." Gil smirked in her direction as his eyes remained on the fight, so he missed her glare and the finger she raised.

"Is everyone okay?" she asked.

Gil nodded. "A few extra holes, but they'll be fine."

A crunch interrupted them. Adelaide tensed. The blue creature's mouth, filled with razor teeth, had closed around the Cradesion's head, snapping it off.

"Fuck! I wouldn't want to meet that thing in a dark alley," Gil said.

Adelaide eyed him. "What about here?"

"How about *you* go out there," Gil muttered under his breath.

She laughed quietly, pulling out a knife from her boot.

"You gonna tickle it?" Gil commented, his lips pulling up in the corner.

"Oh, shut up." It was her turn to mutter.

The creature chewed on its reward for a while before spitting it out. Biting a leg It dragged the body away, leaving the crushed head.

By the time they strode out of the forest, Taurian was barking orders while pressing a hand over the wound on his side. Blue blood dripped through his fingers colouring his tan pants.

She swore, moving quickly in his direction.

"What the hell, Taurian! That needs to be taken care of." She tugged his hand away. A gaping hole marred his torso. Bile rose in her throat. How in the hell was he still standing? "Fuck. Fuck. Gil, where is the portable medical unit?" she yelled as Taurian just stood smirking at her. "What is wrong with you?" she demanded, wondering why no one was helping.

"Here." Cullen handed her the small, rectangular unit.

She slapped it against Taurian's side, making him wince.

"I am glad you care, but our bodies process pain differentially than humans." He pulled off the unit, handing it back.

"It's not done," she protested, eyes wide staring at the open wound, smaller but still there. "And why didn't I know about this ability? Why would you not want the wound fixed?"

"Because it is a need to know." Taurian's intense gaze encompassed the three of them. "I am Tu'val. If it is not life threatening, once the battle is won, I will see the doctor."

"What ability?" Gil responded.

Taurian turned away without answering. "We need to proceed. Time has moved too quickly."

"Did you eliminate the threats?" Adelaide searched the area for bodies.

"One was in the trees; another came from behind. How was your hunt?"

She grinned. "Didn't have to break a sweat. Let's find the last of the bastards so we can blow this place."

They strode across the hard earth towards the waiting mountains. What the fuck was with caves and those bastards? Grumbling, Adelaide scanned the grey rocks, searching for enemies.

Taurian stepped closer, giving a wince.

She glanced his way, trying not to let her worry show. Dumbass should have kept the unit on longer. No matter how good the Tu'Val healing was.

When he swung his arm out, blocking her path, she halted. He raised a finger to his lips. Everyone stood silently.

Adelaide strained her ears but heard nothing.

"I still can not confirm the number of enemies." Taurian whispered, shifting his weight to the right. Adelaide glanced down to his side before meeting his gaze with a raised brow. No way would she suggest he stay behind.

"Not happening," he stated.

"Fine, kill yourself." She had no desire to admit the reason for wanting him to be safe. She would maybe consider bringing it out later to examine. Until then, it was under lock and key. It was possible she'd throw the key away.

"Could they have set up their dampeners?" Gil asked, stepping up beside Adelaide.

"Not sure." Adelaide shrugged. "Good assumption though since it blocks all scanners." She eyed the men, a shiver running down her spine. "We're going in blind."

Everyone swore. Sweat formed on her forehead as flashbacks from her captivity ran through her mind. Shaking it off, Adelaide stepped forward. No way were those motherfuckers getting under her skin. Behaving as a victim wasn't in her DNA. A breakdown once in awhile, yeah. But total paralyses? Nope.

The group moved as one through the cavern opening before fanning out. Creden held his blaster in one hand, his sword in the other. Adelaide would need to use two hands to heft that behemoth.

A putrid smell hit her. Gagging, she held a hand over her nose.

"What the hell is making the stench?" Cullen demanded.

"Smells like a pile of corpses," Gil answered shaking is head. "I wonder if we're going to find some of the locals. Seems like their MO."

They converged on the only tunnel. Following Taurian, Adelaide strained her eyes in the dark, trailing her hand along the wall as a guide. Something tore into her skin, and she jerked her hand away, blood welling along her palm. "Fucker!"

Creden chuckled softly behind her; she turned with a glare before continuing. It was about ten minutes of walking before the Cradesion chittering sounded loud and clear ahead of them. The stench was palpable.

Moving silently, they converged on their targets. A click sounded in Adelaide's head. "About fucking time," she muttered.

"What is it?" Gil asked.

"The translator decided to finally be useful."

"What are they saying?" Taurian demanded.

"They're talking about some type of incendiary device."

"Where?" Cullen glanced around. "What type?"

"Not sure. The translation is spotty." She tilted her head, listening to the conversation. "Sounds like on their ships."

Taurian swore. "How destructive?"

"Total." Her eyes widened, a gasp escaping her lips.

"Hurry, let us kill these nedyetfd and get back to the shuttle," Taurian said.

"Why didn't they use it up there?" Cullen asked, gesturing skyward.

"They haven't said. I'm guessing it isn't complete yet. They're talking about parts. Aren't you hearing this?" she asked.

"Yes. I just wanted to make you tell it all." He grinned at her, ducking as her fist came at him.

"Enough," said Taurian.

"What's the plan?" Cullen whispered.

"We destroy," Taurian answered with a feral grin. He stepped into the cavern.

Bloody wonderful. Adelaide strode behind, studying the green-covered walls. She wrinkled her nose as a wave of sour, putrid air rose from where several Cradesions stood.

Laser fire streaked in their direction, and Adelaide dove to the rocky ground. When she turned her head, she was eye-to-eye-socket with a decomposed head. Biting back a scream, she scrambled to the right, returning fire.

As everyone spread out, advancing on their enemy, Taurian and Creden bellowed a war cry. They charged forward, Taurian slightly ahead, holding his glowing sword in front of his body. His injuries didn't seem to slow him down at all.

Adelaide skirted the edges, aiming to take them from the rear. Gil grunted a few paces to the left. A wail filled the cavern. Adelaide dropped to the ground. Guess she wasn't going unnoticed.

"Move it!" Gil yelled. A loud explosion came from above, pebbles falling over her prone form.

Swearing, she rolled to the right, springing up just as a large piece of the ceiling crashed. Debris ricocheted from the ground as plumes of dust filled the air. Adelaide doubled over, coughing. Screeching echoed, followed by a lot of swear words. Adelaide stumbled, windmilling her arms to stay upright. Her eye caught sight of something. *What the hell*? *Don't look down, don't look down*. But of course, she had to. Multiple body parts littered the cavern floor, and she had just stepped in a thick pool of blood and biofluids.

Swallowing her bile, Adelaide worked her way around, watching for a target. A black form crouched behind a rock, aiming at Cullen. Deciding a laser gun would be noisier and could cause a cave-in, she ran pulling out her sword and swinging for the neck. The creature turned, quickly firing.

Guess they didn't care about bringing the place down, Adelaide thought as she ducked, aiming for the leg. The sword glanced off it's armour as it danced to the left, reaching with another arm towards her sword.

"Not bloody likely." She snarled using her body weight to cut through the digits holding the laser.

An unholy screech left its mouth as black blood gushed from the wound. While it weaved around its other three arms, Adelaide looked for an opening. Two arms grabbed knives from its back and began swinging. Sounds of the surrounding battle reached Adelaide, she resisted checking the statis of the others and concentrated on dodging the swipes aimed at her head. She liked it right where it was.

"Fucker!" she yelled as its right lower arm reached in, slicing her leg. A few trickles of blood dripped, joining the other fluids mixed on the ground. Her sword wasn't doing anything other than scratching up the armour. What the hell was it made of?

They danced a few more minutes before the opening she was waiting for appeared. Swinging across, she made contact. The body dropped with the head rolling away. Breathing deeply, Adelaide bent over, checking her leg. Right now, at least, it was just a sting; after the adrenalin left, it might be more. Searching the cavern, she spotted one creature fighting an enraged Taurian. Three bodies lay on the ground. Where was the other? Clenching her laser and sword, she moved quickly, reaching a good position, where she fired on the creature, knowing she may have a ticked-off Taurian on her hands. He didn't need help, blah blah blah. The thing dropped, and Taurian cleaved the Cradesion's head clean off. Adelaide ran forward, catching sight of Creden on the ground not too far from Taurian.

"I am glad you are alive, Red," Taurian called to her as he knelt beside his soldier.

"What happened? Where are Gil and Cullen?" she demanded.

Taurian gently closed Creden's eyes, then glanced up. "Gil followed the enemy down the tunnel, and Cullen has fallen."

Close to the tunnel Gil had gone down, lay a body. She ran over and shook Cullen's shoulder while searching his prone form for injuries. "Cullen are you alive?" No response came.

"Damn it!" She peered at the tunnel, heaving a sigh of frustration. "And why did Gil go alone? The dampener is still active."

Taurian shrugged. "Because he is a warrior. I will search for him while you guard the bodies."

Adelaide held in her protest. The Tu'Val placed great honor on those who watched the dead. But it was her job to protect Gil. She placed her fingers on Cullen's neck, sighing with relief when a faint pulse beat beneath her finger. She nodded for Taurian to go. He took off while she rolled Cullen over, searching for the cause of his impairment.

"Fucking hell." Adelaide shuddered at the burn winding across the side of his head above his ear. Crouching over the bodies, she faced the cavern entrance, weapon raised. She hoped no one came from the tunnel behind her, but she'd be ready if they did.

It felt like hours before shuffling came from the tunnel behind. She spun around, heart beating rapidly.

"I can fucking walk by myself!" Gil's grumbling voice reached her ears.

Grinning, Adelaide stood, peering into the dark. "Gil! Thank God you're alright." She breathed deep, holding back the urge to envelope Gil in a hug. Taurian didn't look too bad himself as he limped beside Gil, who stumbled into the cavern cradling his arm.

"I'm fine. The scum is dead." Gil glanced to the two bodies she stood over.

"Cullen is holding on by a thread. We need to get out of here," Adelaide said.

"Agreed." Taurian stepped forward, wheezing as he bent down. "I will carry Creden; you can take Cullen."

Adelaide clenched her jaw. How was Taurian going to carry a body when he could barely bend over? A Tu'Val needed their death ceremony for the person to move on, he wouldn't be left behind. She gently pulled Cullen's body closer, praying she didn't damage him further. With Gil's help, they had Cullen's body over her shoulders in a fireman's pose. Steeling herself, she rose into a wide stance.

"Okay, I'm ready." She glanced at Taurian who stood, giving the impression Creden weighed nothing, the jerk. Her body trembled under her load, but there was no way in hell she was dropping him. Stepping carefully, she followed Gil out of the cave. *Good riddance.*

"You didn't find anything back there?" Adelaide asked.

"Not from the quick glance. I have no idea what they were doing here. Maybe scouting for a new location," Gil answered shuffling in front.

Stopping at the entrance, Gil glanced at his comm unit. "Taurian, are you calling for pickup?" he asked.

Taurian nodded. "I am getting no response." He frowned. "Something must be happening." He tried again with no luck. "We will walk until I can reach one of the shuttles."

"You didn't see any dampeners back there?" she questioned again.

"No, nothing." Gil turned. "Maybe they're getting better at hiding them." He shrugged then winced.

Slowly trudging onward, Adelaide hoped they didn't run into any hostiles, or they would be screwed. No way the three of them would be able to defend themselves plus the two extra bodies. She shook her head—Cullen was going to make it. At least she could feel his faint breath on her neck. It was giving her the creeps.

They slogged through the grass, not caring about leaving a trail. Their goal was to reach safety quickly where it was defensible. Sweat sheened on her skin. Stopping for a moment, she searched for disaster, but found nothing.

"Are you going to make it, Red? I did not think you were a quitter," Taurian said, goading her.

Adelaide snarled. "I'll go as long as you do. Just resting a moment." She shifted Cullen, examining his face for signs of life. Putting one foot in front of the other, her body protesting, she reached the others.

"Still no response?" she asked.

"No. Not from either shuttle."

"What about the ships?"

"I will not bring any other ship here until we know the situation."

A rustling to their left had Adelaide swearing. "Come on, give us a break!" she whispered as Gil moved to cover them.

They halted. Adelaide struggled to draw her laser as the grass waved. After more noises and shuffles, a small, furry, yellow creature emerged.

"Aaah, is it ever cute," Adelaide cooed.

Both men eyed her with disgust before turning back, glaring at the fuzzball.

"Come on. Look at his little round feet and fuzzy tail. I could squeeze that little ball."

Taurian snorted, shifting his stance.

Before Adelaide could blink, the cute thing opened a set of chompers, flew across the ground attaching to Gil's leg.

"What the hell!" Gil started jumping around shaking his leg furiously. "Get it off!"

Adelaide erupted with laughter. Even Taurian grinned.

"You fuckers, quit laughing and shoot it!"

"Then stop moving; we might hit you." Adelaide steadied her shaking arm.

"I think it's too the bone. You try standing still." Gil ground his teeth. "Why aren't you helping!" he demanded of Taurian.

"Because Red can do it. Hurry up; Creden is getting heavy."

Gil sighed, stopping in place. He held out his leg. "I'm going to die." Small drops of blood dripped to the ground.

"Hey, I can always leave him with you. We can have a pet on the ship." She smirked.

Gil glared at her, making her grin larger. Adelaide would have waited longer, but Taurian's wound was worrying her. A red beam hit the creature. Red guts and gore flew everywhere, coating Gil's legs.

"For bloody sakes!" Gil shook his leg, a snarl on his lips.

Adelaide shrugged. "You're fine. Let's go so we can check out your boo-boos."

Gil swore and muttered as he limped away.

Pay back is a bitch. Adelaide smirked remembering when she first joined the Zoo. When they had taken cargo to Zartuth, the crew never warned her about the vampire mosquito birds that came out at night. They starred in her nightmares for awhile.

Cresting the rise, she spotted smoke. "What the hell!" Adelaide picked up the pace. Jagged pieces of their shuttle littered the ground.

Taurian gently laid Creden down, then ran to the one remaining shuttle door yelling for the doctor.

"Gil, stay with them." Adelaide ordered before sprinting after Taurian, squeezing past the fallen metal.

"Fuck!" she winced grabbing the top of her head, glaring up at the sharp framework. She grimaced when she pulled her blood coated fingers away.

Taurian's voice echoed ahead. She hoped he'd found the doctor and Shavel still alive. If this was a Cradesion attack they were probably specimens already.

Weaving to the front of the shuttle Adelaide reached the doors and found Taurian trying to force them open.

"We might be able to find something more appropriate than your hands."

He grunted forcing his hands farther into the space. The muscles bulged down his arms and across his shoulders The doors groaned as they slowly opened.

Snapping her mouth shut, Adelaide swiped her face, making sure there was no drool.

When there was adequate room to squeeze through, Taurian stepped back looking over his shoulder.

"That was quicker." He pushed into the room, giving a small groan.

Adelaide frowned at the blue left on the door and had to step over the blood puddle; Taurian needed that wound fixed.

"What happened?" he growled.

The doctor glanced up, his hands pressing against Shavel's stomach.

"I was treating Shavel's wounds when the shuttles alerts sounded. We were bombarded."

"Why was the shuttle not destroyed?" Taurian stepped closer, pushing a fallen beam away.

The doctor smirked. "I was able to activate the shield to cloak our life signs."

Kneeling at Shavel's side, Taurian nodded "Is he going to make it? We lost Creden."

Sadness passed over the doctor's face as he took a deep breath. "He is stable now. If we can get him treatment, he should recover. It will probably be long with intensive therapy."

Taurian smiled. "He needs to build strength and patience. It will be good for him."

The doctor snorted as he stood.

"Are we calling in the calvary now?" Adelaide demanded.

"I will try contacting the other shuttle first to have them assist with retrieval of the wounded."

Adelaide stared at him in surprise. "What about us?" she waved her hands wildly. "You need treatment. So does everyone else."

"There are more enemies on this planet. We will find and eradicate all that are here." He snarled. "No one attacks my people and lives to talk about it. You and your crew can go with the wounded if necessary. Tu'val do not leave enemies behind to attack later."

Adelaide shook her head. "I'm not leaving you alone. We'll send Cullen with the doc. Gil and I will follow you. We want payback."

"Commander, if I may." The doctor stepped forward, eyes downcast, holding a portable regenerator. "I can at least close your wounds."

"Fine. But make it quick." He slowly pulled the bloody shirt over his head.

Adelaide coughed to cover her gasp as she stared at Taurian's green muscled chest. Even with the multiple cuts and blood, he was still gorgeous.

Jerking her eyes away, she stared at the destroyed seats before looking back at Taurian. She frowned at his knowing smirk.

"How about I retrieve any weapons that survived." Adelaide didn't wait for a response before stomping off. Taurian's laughter followed her.

Muttering to herself, she tried to think of all the cons associated with Taurian. She was coming up blank, so not good. The ship groaned and shifted. Sparks flew to her right, and a large crash caused her to dive to the side. She screamed as a sharp pain traveled up her leg. A thin metal shard stuck out of her calf.

"What the fuck!"

A large section of the ceiling hung down, covering most of the area. The panel with the weapons hung just beyond the collapse.

Clenching her teeth, Adelaide forced the yell back as she turned over and grabbed the piece of metal. She hesitated. Maybe pulling it out wasn't a smart idea. Looking at the debris, she yanked. The pain was excruciating. Spots danced in front of her eyes. Breathing deeply, Adelaide tried to stay awake as she pressed against the wound. Blood seeped through her fingers. Surprised no one responded to her yells, she prepared to stand. She couldn't just lie there. Taurian would probably step over her, stating he couldn't wait for her. A little giggle escaped her lips. Yes, time to move. She was not going to mention that she received a grievous wound from the ship, no battle around.

Her eyes roamed over her pants. She grinned at a tear at the bottom of the left leg. Pulling hard, she ripped off a strip, which she wrapped around her newest wound. The others were already crusted over and could wait for the doctor. Adelaide placed her hand on the ledge beside and heaved her body up.

"Holy crap!" she grimaced, stumbling against the wall. What she wouldn't give for a pain patch.

Hobbling forward, she ducked under the panel. When she reached the side wall, she pushed the button and waited. "Damn it" After several jabs, the panel finally slid open. Adelaide stretched her hand into the hole, feeling for any weapons. Jackpot! She pulled out three lasers then glanced behind her, wondering what was taking Taurian so long. Brow furrowed, she stuffed the treasures into the available pockets on her jacket and headed to the exit. Outside, she shielded her eyes and searched for Gil.

"What the hell happened to you?" Gil's voice made Adelaide jump.

"Don't do that!" she yelled. Pain radiated through her body as her damaged leg landed.

Gil smirked, pointing to her injury. "Your one of us now. Is Taurian's body somewhere in there?" he gestured to the mutilated pile of metal.

Adelaide glanced back at the shuttle. "I left him and the doctor to grab all the weapons."

"What's the plan?" Gil asked, slowly lowering to the ground with a grunt. His eyes strayed to Cullen's still form.

"Taurian will try contacting the other shuttle for a retrieval to take the injured back to the ship. We three will hunt down the Cradesions."

A beep on Adelaide's comm had them both looking down.

"Who is it?" Gil asked.

Adelaide grimaced. "The General." She disconnected the call. "What?" she demanded as Gil smirked. "I don't have time to deal with his bullshit. I'll send a report when we complete this mission."

They both turned at a noise coming from the shuttle. Taurian squeezed through the opening, carrying Shavel. The doctor followed behind, maneuvering the floating table. He wrestled it sideways, shoving it in front of him through the opening and swearing when it got stuck. Adelaide started in his direction but was waved off.

"I have this." He grunted.

Shavel's grumbles reached Adelaide's ears, and she tried not to grin. She could imagine the warrior's opinion about being carried by his commander.

Once everything was situated, the doctor fussed with Shavel, settling him on the table before turning his observant eyes on everyone else. "I will look over each of you while the Commander is contacting the other shuttle."

"We have a portable unit," Gil said. "You don't need to worry."

"I am a qualified doctor. I will assess each of you. Our equipment is superior."

Taurian stepped farther away, his gait seeming more at ease. The doctor moved to Cullen, bending down to place the scanner on Cullen's forehead. The machine beeped for a few minutes before the holodisplay showed the results. Muttering under his breath, the doctor pulled more tools from his pocket.

Adelaide moved closer. "Is he going to be alright?"

"He has a lot head trauma."

"And?" she demanded when the doctor paused.

He glanced back. "He should make a full recovery once the bleeding is taken care of. Now quiet, I have to work."

Adelaide mimed zippering her lips as she collapsed to the ground, exhaustion setting in. Her eye lids drooped as the doctor stood.

"I have done all I can." He headed toward Gil who shook his head." Enough. You are a grown man. Do not act like a child."

Gil frowned but allowed him to poke and prod.

Adelaide laughed. "You tell him Doc. I can't get him to do anything."

"I wouldn't talk, Captain," Gil growled. He flinched as the animal bites were disinfected and sealed. When the torture was finished, the doctor slapped a med patch on Gil's arm.

"You are next." The doctor eyed Adelaide. "Are you going to give me trouble?"

"No sir. I don't like bleeding out."

Gil snorted. "I don't think your on-death's door."

Adelaide glared at Gil as the doctor bent down to examine her. "Why is Cullen still out?" she asked.

"His body must heal. I repaired the damage."

Taurian returned, addressing the doctor, "Red alright?"

"Yes, Commander."

"Did you contact them?" Adelaide asked.

"Yes. They are on the opposite side of the planet. The shuttle they followed landed by multiple caves."

"Are they able to evac us?"

"Yes."

"Are we just supposed to sit out in the open waiting for an attack?"

Taurian huffed as his gaze turned to the way they had travelled. "There is not cover available. We will move closer to the shuttle and hope our signatures will be harder to detect. I do not want to chance the shuttle collapses with us inside."

Adelaide slowly stood. "Let's go, old man." She gestured at Gil. "Help me move Cullen."

They all settled in to wait for a rescue, which pissed her off. She was getting tired of being one step behind. "Can I make a suggestion?" she asked.

"What?" Taurian barked.

She held her breath a moment so she didn't blurt out the first thing that wanted to spew out. "Why don't I contact the Clandestine. They can help us with the Cradesions. I'm sure my little ship won't make much difference to the fight compared to your war ships up there."

"The ship will be an asset." Taurian stared at her for a moment before nodding.

She grinned, pushing her comm to call the Clandestine.

"I wish we were able to search the Cradesion shuttle. We might be able to discover something useful." Adelaide said tracking Taurian's movements.

"We can not separate at this time. I do not want to give the enemy more time than necessary to disappear." Taurian frowned staring at the sky.

*   *   *

The faint hum of an engine came from their left. They all crouched with weapons raised, waiting for confirmation if it was the enemy or the friendlies.

A sigh escaped between Adelaide's clenched teeth as their shuttle came into view.

"I hope it's our men piloting," Gil muttered under his breath.

It stopped, hovering a moment before slowly setting down. The door slid open revealing Taurian's men. The warriors hurried the two injured men onto the shuttle and had to physically push the stubborn doctor as well.

"They need you," Taurian growled. "I do not have to be coddled."

The doctor's shoulders slumped. "Yes, Commander." He turned and strode into the shuttle.

Taurian gave a few more commands to his men before stepping back. The shuttle zoomed away.

Adelaide prayed that Cullen would recover. Turning towards Taurian, she asked, "What is the plan?"

"I will study the data and determine a plan. We will move as close as their sensors allow, monitoring their movements. We will find a weakness and strike."

Gil grinned. "I can get behind that. We have the fire power on board to do some damage."

"The Clandestine is here." Adelaide interrupted, knowing Taurian was going to make a comment and piss off Gil.

Chapter 12

Adelaide smiled as she stared around the bridge, glad to be back. "Has the scan been completed yet?"

"It's just coming up, Captain," Gil responded.

The bridge was silent as they all studied the display. The Cradesions must have their dampener_ activated because the ship sensors weren't showing any life signs. But it could detect the environment.

Adelaide turned as the door to the bridge slid open.

Edward walked in, stopping to gawk at the screen. "Those have to be rocks, right?" he asked.

"How were they able to make all those structures?" Adelaide whispered.

"I don't know. Until we can disable their dampeners, we're running blind," Gil said.

Taurian grinned. "We drop a couple of bombs, that will solve our problems."

"What the hell, Taurian?" Adelaide yelled. "There could be hostages down there."

"You really think we can fight effectively down in those caves?" Taurian pointed at the screen.

"We were able to on Tikaani, and we saved the captives."

"You were captured and tortured." He snarled. "How many of the creatures were there? I do not think it will be close to how many are here."

Adelaide wanted to argue more but knew Taurian was right about numbers. But she couldn't condone blowing everything up with out investigating. "I'll agree, but first I'm sneaking in to confirm numbers and if there are hostages," she stated.

They all started arguing at once. *Men.* She snorted.

"You're not going down there by yourself." Gil glared at her.

"I'm going. If you gentlemen are too scared to go, I'll be good on my own." She smirked as Taurian swore, pacing in front of her chair.

"Stop it, Taurian. You're making me dizzy."

He whipped his head around, lip pulled back in a snarl. Gil stepped closer to her chair as everyone watched Taurian.

"I will not harm Red, but the rest of you are fair game."

Adelaide let out a loud sigh. "Boys, boys. Keep it together. Does that mean you're all accompanying me? Yeah!" Grinning, she clapped her hands.

"I give up." Gil threw up his hands. "You can have her." He stomped off the bridge.

"Eh! I should be insulted," Adelaide yelled.

The others on the bridge laughed.

"Did you hear that, Red. We have Gil's permission." Taurian stalked towards her.

Adelaide jumped up shaking her head, "Nope, I don't think that's what he meant. Gil!"

Taurian stepped in front, grabbed her arms and yanked her forward. Their lips met, and his arms tightened around her. It didn't take long before she softened and began to enthusiastically participate. Whistle calls penetrated the fog around Adelaide, causing her to quickly pull away.

"Would you quit doing that?" She glared at Taurian.

He smirked. "If I give you warning, you have the chance to run."

"Well duh."

This isn't good, she thought, trying not to shiver. An intriguing look showed in his eyes.

"Mmmm. I will keep that in mind." He stepped past her, walking towards the door.

"Wait, what? What does that mean?" Adelaide demanded as he left.

He didn't respond.

She really felt like stomping her foot but restrained herself because five pairs of eyes were glued to her. Snarling, she spun around. "Show's over. Let's get ready." She slammed her hand on the console, and her voice echoed throughout the ship: "We're leaving in ten minutes. If you're not in the cargo bay, I'm leaving you behind." Finished with the command, Adelaide hurried from the bridge to her quarters. She needed to raid her weapons stash. Taurian had confiscated the weapons she found on the shuttle.

The door slid shut behind her as she rushed around the bed. A buzzing on her wrist distracted her, and she smacked her hip against the corner of the table.

"Fuck, fuck." She rubbed her side and checked her wrist comm. With a grimace, Adelaide accepted the call.

The general's face came into view. It wasn't happy. "Where have you been? Why were you ignoring my call?"

"Sorry, General. We were in the middle of a battle." She held herself very still so her distaste didn't show on her face.

"Those weren't your orders." His face turned a mottled red.

"You told me to observe sir. That is what I was doing. There was no way I would take the Clandestine into the middle of the battle and chance capture or death."

The general took a deep breath. "What do you have to report?"

"The Tu'Val engaged the Cradesion ships and destroyed most of them, and the other ships ran."

He looked surprised. "They had enough fire power to penetrate the ships hulls?"

"Yes. I told you sir that we need to make friends with the Tu'val. We need them."

"No. I want you to find the plans for their ships so we can use their technology."

Adelaide's mouth opened and closed as she regarded the general. "I'm not a spy. I am a captain. I will not behave in such a manner to a potential ally and our saviours. They rescued us from torture and death." Her mouth tightened and her fists clenched. *What the hell was going on at Earth central? No way in hell was she going to do that.*

"You will be retrieving the information for your people, or you will be declared an enemy of the state. It is up to you," the general snarled.

Adelaide almost gave him the finger and told him to fuck off. Closing her eyes for a moment, she said through clenched teeth, "Of course, General. I'm not sure how long it will take."

"We need that information quickly. Don't take too long." The screen went black.

"Fucking bastards. What the fuck!" Adelaide paced back and forth. She needed to calm down. They were all probably waiting for her. She would deal with this after.

Gil and his cronies were all waiting with wide grins, which were dropped when she stepped into the cargo bay. She was sure frustration and menace flowed out from her. No time for chit chat. Taurian straightened from his place against the wall, eyes trained on her.

"Okay we are going in quick and quiet," she barked. "No unnecessary talking." She marched to the door.

Gil looked at her questioningly, but she shook her head slightly.

Taurian frowned. "That is not how you wage war. You don't leave enemies behind you."

She whipped around to glare. "Moments ago, you said there would be tons down there and it's too dangerous."

"Yes," he said slowly. "Now we are venturing into their domain, so we must exterminate."

"Ahhh!" Adelaide threw up her hands. "No! Unless we are caught, no killing. It could alert others. Does everyone have enough weapons? There are more in the locker over there." She pointed to the corner as they all nodded. "We should be taking the night goggles." She grabbed enough for everyone, but Taurian declined.

"Okay, let's go." She opened the doors, and they filed out.

Adelaide glanced down at the map on her holodisplay. "It should only be about a twenty-minute hike to the cave entrance." She glanced at the darkening skies. "Taurian, do you want to lead since your eyesight is better than ours even with the goggles?"

"Yes." Taurian stepped in front and headed in the direction of the caves.

They were all silent, weapons drawn, eyes scanning their surroundings. Dread settled in the pit of Adelaide's stomach. Hopefully she wasn't leading anyone to their deaths. The tall grass brushed against her waist causing a shiver to run down her back. Creatures had better not be lurking out there, unseen.

She was counting on everything keeping their distance from the Cradesions.

As they neared their destination, Taurian held up his hand and crouched behind a large boulder.

"What is it?" Adelaide whispered, kneeling beside Taurian and adjusting her goggles.

"I saw movement." Their waiting was rewarded when a shape separated from the black night, shifting to the left.

"Can I kill it?" Taurian asked.

"Fine, but make sure you hide the body."

Taurian narrowed his eyes at her. "You think I do not know about proper disposal?" he snarled.

"Sorry, I know you do. Just hurry."

Taurian was gone, disappearing into the darkness. Adelaide held her breath, waiting for him to come back to her.

It didn't take long before Taurian was slinking back through the tall grass. She shook her head in wonder. How could such a big guy move so silently? She looked back at Connor, another large and silent killer. There was only slight movement to the grass as he stepped beside her. Connor touched her arm lightly. "How's it going kiddo?" he whispered

"Alright." She took a deep breath. "It will be."

Connor nodded then turned to watch for Taurian.

Taurian drew to her side. Dots of the Cradesion's black blood speckled his arm.

"Everything good?" she asked.

Giving a grunt, he led them forward.

Small dark blobs sat on either side of the cave entrance. When Adelaide stepped, a faint crunch sounded. Lifting her foot, she saw a crushed bone. It had better be from an animal, or she might be sick. It seemed to be a running theme with these things. A nest of bones anywhere they were.

They split apart, approaching on both sides of the entrance, where they froze, weapons drawn.

Straining her ears, Adelaide lifted her wrist. "Nothing now. What do you think we'll find?" she whispered.

"Battle with worthy opponents," Taurian answered.

She sighed, no point in reminding him about the plan. She was surprised Taurian even agreed to try and be stealthy. It was ingrained in every Tu'Val to destroy any threat to their species.

Taurian entered first, motioning everyone to follow.

See one cave, see them all, Adelaide thought. Shivers ran through her body as their boots made splashes. She had no intention of peering down to confirm it was only water. She learnt that mistake in the last cave.

It was silent as they moved deeper into the earth. Hopefully if there were hostages, they would be able to rescue them without any casualties on their side.

Eventually, movement occurred ahead, and everyone froze, eyes peering into the darkness. Advancing slowly to a small opening, Adelaide jostled beside Taurian, staring into the cavern. She swore softly, dread filling her.

"We are not leaving them," Taurian growled, gripping his sword.

There appeared to be at least a hundred Cradesions moving around the vast cavern. A large cone-shaped rock formation in the middle reached to the ceiling. It was littered with holes, which the creatures were moving in and out of. Pathways ran along the cavern walls with more openings, and at the bottom the creatures appeared to be in the process of building multiple war ships.

"How in the hell will they get those out of here?" Albert whispered.

"Where are all the slaves?" Gil asked.

"I don't know. Maybe they don't use them for this purpose, but only as incubators or for menial labor. This is the first time I've seen the ships," Adelaide answered. "What about you?" She turned to Taurian, almost taking a step back. His lip was curled in a snarl and death peered at her through his vivid purple eyes.

"We will leave the cavern and contact my fleet to destroy this location. What do you mean incubators?"

"I'll explain later. What about the survivors?" Adelaide demanded.

"We are not going to allow the enemy to escape. Waiting till we confirm survivors is not acceptable. I am in charge of this mission. We leave now," Taurian snarled, spinning around.

Albert raised his brow at her, waiting. Adelaide knew there was nothing she could do except leave.

Nodding, she followed Taurian out. He checked comms constantly until his signal reached the fleet.

Adelaide listened as Taurian commanded two of his warships to fire on their location. "We must leave now!"

Rocks fell above them as part of the ceiling exploded. They all spun, behind them stood approximately eight Cradesions encased in armour.

"Shit, shit!" Adelaide yelled. "Fire at the ceiling and run like hell." She grunted as pain flared in her side. Trying to ignore the wound, she fired while following the others. Once she had dodged out of the cave, there came a loud crack, and large pieces of rock landed in front of the entrance. Ear-piercing screeches cut through the air as they ran for their lives. Adelaide stumbled as her leg began ignoring her orders.

"Red! Move it." Worry filled Taurian's face.

Laser fire flew past, and she stopped. "I'll hold them while you get the others back." She yelled kneeling behind an outcrop.

"We aren't leaving without you!" Gil growled.

"That's an order. Someone needs to warn Earth, and I'm already injured. Get to the ship and come rescue me."

Albert grabbed Gil's arm with a nod and dragged him forward.

Taurian knelt beside her with a grin. "What a way to go." Blood dripped from a gash on his forehead, and his side was leaking again.

Quite a pair we make, she thought.

A large plume of smoke exited the cave followed by a loud crash. Adelaide swore as two Cradesions appeared at the entrance. "Here they come," she yelled, firing. "How much longer till your ships arrive?"

Exploding debris flew past them, some pieces making contact. Glancing up, she saw the two ships emerge from the dark, swirling clouds. The cannons fired, and a moment, later the ground shook as a large crater appeared beside the cave.

"Run! Run! I'm not giving up." Adelaide grabbed Taurian's arm.

They stumbled together as the ground heaved, crevices forming behind and in front of them. Rocks thundered as they rolled into the abyss. Screeches echoed into the night as they weaved towards freedom, trying to dodge the laser fire. Adelaide's breath came out in pants, her body aching everywhere and her leg going numb. She didn't think Taurian was doing much better, but he'd never admit it. It was so tempting to give up and lay down, but there was no way she was giving those jackasses the satisfaction. Coughing as the dust encased them, she felt the burn in her lungs. With her arm, she covered her mouth and pushed herself faster, trying not to slow Taurian down. They crested a hill and spotted the Clandestine. The ship was hovering as the ground shook beneath.

"How much fire power did your guys use?" Adelaide snarled; this was a long reach. "Get us out of here!" she cried into the comm.

Seconds later, they both appeared in the cargo bay. Adelaide collapsed, deciding this was a good spot to die. The engine hummed as the ship shot into space.

Chapter 13

Footsteps pounded on the floor.

"Captain, are you dead?" Bato smirked as he knelt in front of Adelaide's face.

She slowly held up her middle finger. "I am hard to kill. Ask Gil."

Taurian snorted beside her. "Red would stay alive just to spite you. Dock with my ship; they are expecting us."

Gil reached tugging Adelaide up. "Let's get you to med bay. You look like shit. Commander, are you coming?"

"Yes, I better keep an eye on her in case she tries to escape."

"Hardy har. I can't move. Therefore, the first bed I see will be where my body collapses."

"We must wait then until we are aboard my ship, and I can take you too my quarters." Taurian smirked as he grabbed her arm.

She groaned as her body trembled in pain. "I probably would if it were closer." Adelaide ignored

Taurian's surprised look and smile, but Gil was watching him with narrowed eyes.

When they reached the med bay, the door slid open, and the med bot came into view.

"How can I be of service?"

"The captain needs patched up," Gil said.

"Please remove your clothing and get into the scanning unit."

"Everyone out!" Adelaide demanded.

"Yup I'm gone." Gil said practically running out of the room.

"I am not leaving. You need help." Taurian crossed his arms, glaring at her.

"Fine. But it'll be good just to my underwear."

Taurian grinned, moving closer. "You can explain about the incubator comment to distract yourself."

"Okay," she said as Taurian helped her remove her jacket. "On Tikaani, we found some of the survivors had been implanted with Cradesion eggs."

Horror crossed Taurian's face. "Where are they?" he demanded, slowly pulling her pants down as she held on to the unit.

"We have them hidden on the Clandestine."

"What about Earth?"

"They weren't interested in helping. They have demanded we bring them in. The victims would have been kept in isolation so the creatures could hatch," she whispered.

Taurian snarled. "You are going to take them to Earth?"

Adelaide violently shook her head, growling, "Are you fucking kidding me. There is no way in hell I would do that. We have them hidden so that doesn't happen."

"You are not following orders from your superiors?" He eyed her in surprise.

"Whatever." She faced away. "I will not agree to such commands. It is inhumane. No one should be treated like that. I know the Tu'Val wouldn't do this. Can you help?"

Taurian frowned. "Yes, we will not allow the creatures to live. If it is possible to save the victims, we will."

Adelaide gave a small smile. "Thanks. This information can't be released. Need to know, only."

"Agreed." Taurian assisted Adelaide as she slowly lifted her leg and clambered into the unit. She squeaked as the hard bed seemed to suck the heat out of her body.

"We will talk once you are healed."

"What about you?"

"I will be fine until we reach my ship. Do not worry."

The med bot pushed some buttons, and the lid closed, encasing Adelaide. Knowing that he would try and help the victims allowed her to close her eyes and relax slightly as the unit did its job.

*   *   *

Beeping startled Adelaide awake. She cursed as her head smacked the top of the unit. Surprised to hear no laughing outside at her expense, she pushed the disappointment way down when the lid opened and she was able to see into the room.

"Where is Commander Taurian?" she asked the med bot.

"He is not here."

"I know that!" she snarled climbing out of the unit and stomping to the replicator. As she pulled on pants, her brain fired. She grimaced before pressing her comm.

"Gil, where are you?"

"Your alive," Gil said as his frowning face appeared on the screen. "You're not allowed to do that again, or I'll kill you myself."

Adelaide paused before responding. "You know it was the right call, or none of us would be here."

Gil huffed. "Doesn't matter. Glad you're alright."

Adelaide smiled as the med bay door slid open. "What's going on?"

"We're docked on Taurian's ship. We're all patched up thanks to their doc. We've been waiting for you before meeting."

"How are Cullen and Shavel?" she asked.

"Shavel is doing alright." Gil grimaced. "Cullen is doing as well as expected."

"What's that supposed to mean?" Adelaide demanded.

"They've repaired the damage, but he hasn't woken yet."

"Do they expect him too?" She dreaded the answer.

"Yes. It just might take time."

"I'll go check on him shortly. Are you alone?" Adelaide whispered.

"I'm with Edward in engineering."

"I told Taurian."

"What did he say?" Gil asked.

"He'll help to try and save them."

"You believe him?"

"Yes. It's a matter of honor to them once they give their word. I'll contact Taurian, you make sure the ship is ready."

"Sounds good."

The five musketeers were yucking it up but stopped when she walked onto the bridge.

"What?" she demanded.

"Nothing." Albert smirked. "Surprised Taurian isn't with you."

"Why? Did he say something?" she cursed in her head as soon as the words left her mouth. Laughter filled the room, and she growled. "Oh, shut up. I'm off to find Taurian. Be ready. Not sure what the plan is." Adelaide hadn't taken more than a few steps off the Clandestine before she was greeted by a Tu'Val soldier.

"Where can I find Commander Taurian?"

"He is waiting on the bridge. Follow me." He spun around marching through the cargo bay.

"I can make it on my own," she called out but was ignored. Muttering under her breath, she quickly followed. Their steps echoed around the empty bay; the corridors were the same. Where was everyone? When they passed by the gym, grunts and yells echoed.

Adelaide peeked inside. The room was packed with Tu'Val fighting and training. A few of them sported bruises or cuts. She wondered if it was from battle or here.

"Hurry."

"I'm coming."

"He is waiting." The soldier gestured her to continue onto the bridge.

"Thanks." She nodded.

"Red, nice to see you up." Taurian's gaze travelled up her body, probably inspecting for injuries. Just like she was doing to him. She didn't see anymore holes. It was deathly silent. It seemed the crew were watching them closely. She kept her eyes on Taurian, sure her face was turning red.

"I'm good to go. There are some things we need to discuss, Commander."

"Yes. Come with me." Taurian led her to his ready room. The moment the door slid shut Taurian grabbed Adelaide's shoulders yanking her to him. She barely resisted, before her arms crept around his body and she sighed.

"I almost lost you," he whispered.

"Nope, I'm hard to kill." Her voice was muffled against his hard chest. She could feel the quick beat of his heart.

"Okay. Time to get these fuckers." She snarled pulling back slightly.

Taurian's beautiful lips grinned down at her. His hand moved the few strands of her hair away from her face.

"I love when you are blood thirsty." He gave her a quick kiss before moving away, probably expecting her to hit him.

She debated but instead moved to the table and pulled out a chair. "What's the plan? Are we following the fleeing ships?"

"Yes. But we are proceeding with caution. It is probably a trap. I want to see these victims."

Adelaide raised her brow. A blue glow seemed to emanate from him. She'd never seen that before.

"So, are you completely healed?" she asked.

"Yes. The doctor repaired my injuries. Can we please see them?" He seemed to choke on those last few words.

She held back the grin. "Yes. Let's go."

She messaged Gil, and he directed them to the engine room. Every few feet a soldier saluted, and Taurian gave a solemn nod. They seemed to have multiplied. Green muscles everywhere.

Adelaide smirked as Taurian gave her a hard stare anytime, she looked too long.

Grunts and swearing reached their ears. They stepped out of the cargo bay and turned the corner, where they stopped to watch the men spar. Sweat glistened their bodies. She would never say within their hearing, but for their age they were still in great shape.

Their muscles weren't huge bulges but were well defined and rippled as they moved across the floor. She nodded at them before leading Taurian deeper into the ship. She loved the slick rounded curves of the walls, shiny with newness. Taurian was a silent stalker beside her, taking in every tech used.

Adelaide stopped in front of the door to the engine room. "I want to confirm this will go no further. I'm not trying to insult you, but after everything we went through, I'm leery."

When Taurian's lip curled in a snarl, she forced herself not to take a step back, her face blank.

"I should have made them suffer longer; their death was too quick."

"What?" She looked at him in surprise.

"Hurting you is unacceptable."

Warmth filled Adelaide, and a grin threatened to break free. "Let's go." She stepped into the room. The low hum did bring a smile to her face. The lights from the engine brightened the space. She hoped Gil wasn't anywhere near the jump gate. Adelaide wasn't ready to share that tech yet.

"Gil, where are you?" she yelled.

His head popped up from behind a console, his hair dishevelled and a grimace gracing his face.

"Something wrong?"

"Nothing I can't handle, Captain. You brought a guest." Gil regarded Taurian.

"I came to show him our other guests."

"Follow me. Edward, I'll be back."

Edward stepped into sight. "Sounds good." He pushed back his blond hair. "Do you need help?"

"Not right now. I'll let you know," Gil responded, turning away.

Edward nodded before disappearing into the back.

Stepping around the parts lying on the floor, Adelaide wiped the sweat from her forehead and opened her jacket. Glancing at Taurian, she snickered. His eyes were constantly moving.

Gil looked at Taurian before reaching over and punching in the code. A faint glow shone out of the room. Capsule upon capsule covered the floor. They squeezed past the first one. Stopping, Taurian slowly put his hand on the glass, staring at the still form inside. Fury crossed his face.

Tears gathered in Adelaide's eyes, but she blinked them away. The woman had a small extended belly. Her long black hair was matted to her head, her skin was covered in dried dirt and blood.

Taurian gave a low growl.

She put a hand on his arm. "Can you help them?" she asked quietly.

The growl stopped but the fury remained. "How many?" he snarled.

"We found twenty." Gil grimaced.

"We will take them home and plan for war," Taurian announced. "We will arrive tomorrow." He turned to leave.

"I think we need to go elsewhere," Adelaide said.

Taurian slowly turned. "We had a deal," he growled.

Gil turned to Adelaide, but she shook her head. "I know." She held up her hand. "But we need to inform the Syndicate. I don't think Earth has sent them all the information."

'We do not need the Syndicate. There are other allies of the Tu'Val."

"Taurian, we need everyone on board. Yes, the Tu'Val can destroy the Cradesions. But if we are correct about their numbers, we need more."

Taurian snarled, striding away from them.

Adelaide swore hurrying after him. "Taurian, you misunderstand. I'm not asking. I'm telling you."

Gil snorted behind her.

"Shut up, Gil," she said without much heat.

She ran into Taurian's back when he stopped suddenly.

"You will come home first. Then we will discuss."

"Fine."

Taurian stomped away.

"And it's not my home," she called out to his receding back.

Gil laughed, slapping her back. "You sure told him."

"Do you think Earth passed on the information?"

Gil shrugged. "I'm sure they sent most of it. Probably not about the eggs."

Adelaide sighed. "I think you're right."

They headed to the bridge.

"What about the Clandestine?" Gil questioned.

"We don't want to be running for the rest of our lives. I also want our ship back. We might have to leave the Clandestine. I'll think about all the possibilities."

Gil nodded. "We can send out feelers. See what Earth is up to."

"Yes. Let me know what you find out. I need to sleep so I'm alert when we get to Raau."

"You'll need your wits dealing with him." Gil grinned. "You could do worse." He suggested as the bridge door opened.

"She could do worse for what?" Draydon asked, eyebrows wiggling.

"Nothing," she growled.

"We like him," Bato said.

"Who are you talking about?" she asked. "I better get going. Gil will give the update."

Laughter followed her as she stalked away, middle finger raised. "Assholes." It only caused them to laugh louder.

Chapter 14

Adelaide was still exhausted when she peeled her eyes open. Writing the report knocked her out. She could probably sleep a few days. Exhaling, Adelaide ran a hand through her knotted red curls. Time to quite procrastinating and call the General. *Yoo-hoo*, she thought. Stumbling to the replicator she punched in the strongest liquor they had. After downing the red liquid courage, she braced her hands on the wall, head bowed. She breathed deep to calm herself so she would be less likely to yell.

Sitting on the bed, Adelaide connected to the base.

The general appeared. "Status update," he commanded.

Sir. I haven't been able to find specs yet. We are being watched too closely."

"What about their commander?"

"What about him, sir?"

"Could you get closer to him?"

Shock filled Adelaide then anger. "Excuse me, sir? Are you suggesting I whore myself out?" She jumped to her feet.

"Well, no." He frowned. "But if you showed interest, then that might give you another avenue."

"I. Am. Not. Going to do that." Her voice rose as she snarled. "I am a captain in the military. My goal is to ensure the survival of Earth or at least the human race. There may be some who don't deserve to be saved. Sir." Adelaide disconnected before she screamed.

"That mother fucker. What the hell is going on there?" She hadn't really spoken to any of her contacts from her days in the military. Not sure if there was anyone else she could contact there, it appeared that connecting with the Syndicate might be the best course of action.

Gil was even further away from the military, but maybe he knew someone. Once dressed in her standard black pants and shirt, Adelaide hurried from her room. Gil was probably on the Clandestine.

She pressed her comm. "Gil, where are you?"

He responded sounding quite chipper, she frowned.

"Hey, captain. We're in the mess hall."

"Who's we?" she asked suspiciously.

"Just the guys"—a pause— "and Taurian." He laughed.

Oh my God, she thought, breaking into a run. So not good. Were they drinking together? She skidded to a stop in front of the room, staring in horror. Gil, his musketeers, the recruit, Taurian and a few of his officers were sitting around the table, laughing. The reason for their camaraderie sat in front of them. A couple of empty bottles of alcohol. They all tipped back a shot.

"Hey, Red. Did you come to join us?" Taurian winked, probably expecting her to say no.

She gave up. If you can't beat them, join them. Adelaide grabbed a chair and pushed in between Taurian and Cullen. She straddled the seat, grabbed a shot glass and said, "Pour me one. Cullen you look like shit. Are you even breathing?"

"I hear I owe you thanks for carrying me to safety." Cullen's tired eyes studied her. His stringy hair hung beside sunken cheeks. A small smile played across his face.

One of Taurian's men leaned across the table to pour the blue liquid into her glass. It had a strong earthy smell. One of the Tu'Val's famous alcohols, which they didn't usually share.

"What's the occasion?" she asked Taurian as Cullen picked up his shot glass.

"Celebration of a successful battle and to honor fallen comrades."

Adelaide gave a small smile before raising her glass. "To Bastion." Then she swallowed. It had such an overwhelming bite; she barely stopped the grimace.

Taurian grinned. "Another, Red?"

"Keep them coming."

After the last few weeks, she needed to unwind before she had to fight for their lives again.

*   *   *

Adelaide groaned as she rolled over. Clenching her eyes tightly shut she rubbed her forehead. Someone chuckled, and she snarled, knowing who it was. Well, she shot herself in the foot. There was no going back, and she didn't think she wanted to.

"Damn it, Taurian, quit laughing at me. I want some drugs, now!"

The bed jostled. "Come on Red, open those beautiful eyes. We're home. I'll get you something."

Adelaide peeled her lids up, grimacing as the light hit. "How can you be so cheerful?" she demanded.

Taurian's eyes twinkled. "You wanted to prove yourself. I believe you did last longer than everyone except for me. I have been drinking for many more years."

"Move out of the way. I'm going to go die in the shower."

Taurian chuckled as he offered his hand. "Do you want company?"

"Nope. I want to die in peace. You can get me the drugs. Make yourself useful." She yanked on her clothes as she headed for the door.

"You can use my shower." Taurian was watching her stumble away.

"None of my things are here. I need a change of clothes. Once I'm clean I don't want to be wearing these dirty ones." She shuffled into the corridor, swearing at the movement. The breath burst out of her mouth as she collided with a warm body.

"Sorry," Adelaide said, looking up. "Oh crap."

"Having an early visit, Captain?" Cullen grinned.

"Nope." She pushed past, heading to her quarters.

"Wait! That's not an answer."

"Have a nice morning."

* * *

Adelaide watched the screen as the palace grew. The last time she had seen this planet was when Gil rescued her from Taurian. The bastard had kidnapped her. During her escape, Adelaide was almost eaten by a plant. A shiver ran up her back. Not a great feeling. Of course, she was now here by her own free will. Her head needed to be examined. Adelaide chuckled.

Taurian turned towards her. "Care to share?"

"I will probably not venture anywhere near your forest." She crossed her arms, glaring at him.

He grinned. "Come on, you had fun. Admit it."

"Not even going there. I'll be in the cargo bay waiting to disembark."

Mirth filled his face as she turned to leave the bridge.

THE END

OTHER BOOKS BY
YVONNE YOURKOWSKI

YVONNE YOURKOWSKI
SPACE CAPTAIN
ADELAIDE
A CRIME LORD'S DEBT

Family tensions, a missing sibling and the threat of ferocious man-eating aliens complicate her plans and could very well drive Adelaide insane. She must fight on every front to save the family company and keep her brother alive from the threat of a fanatical crime lord. Don't forget about the crazy alien stalker bent on making her his bride.

KAILA PORTER SERIES 1

MURDER
FROM BEYOND
THE GRAVE

YVONNE
YOURKOWSKI

Officer Kaila Porter gasps for breath as she stares at the corpse of her mentor. It has been years since the town, or herself, has seen a dead body. Struggling to move past the devastation, with no clear motive for the vicious attack, Kaila doesn't see the stalker dodging her every step. When the only suspect shows up dead Kaila is plunged into the midst of the criminal world. Suspecting a leak in the department, Kaila strives to connect the two victims, one, a beloved woman of the community, and the other, a newcomer. Kaila finds courage within herself to defy the conspirators who attempt to kidnap her and sabotage the investigation. The town is in an uproar, demanding protection. Time is running out. She must stop the deadly string of murders, before she's next.

KAILA PORTER SERIES 2

SWEETEST REVENGE

YVONNE YOURKOWSKI

The only way to stop the voices is to appease them with more blood, and he's more than capable of obliging.

Detective Kaila Porter can't explain the motive of a brutal stabbing of a young woman, and it's keeping her awake at night. Time is of the essence--bodies start piling up and the murders become increasingly vicious. The worst is believed; a serial killer is on the loose, gaining confidence with every kill.

As the investigation progresses, evidence begins implicating the victims' parents. Is it possible? Kaila can't fathom what would possess parents to kill their own children. There must be a crucial clue they're missing. In desperation Kaila follows their last lead: money. The trail leads to a suspect with the age old motive...Revenge.

KAILA PORTER SERIES **3**

INCINERATED

YVONNE
YOURKOWSKI

Fire cleanses and regenerates life. When arson is used to stop a blackmailer, the pressure mounts. More than one person will be burned.Detective Kaila Porter leaves the scene with blackened nightmares etched into her mind. When investigating the victim brings up more questions then answers, Kaila knows it's time to turn up the heat. Not even an explosion can thwart her determination to reach the truth.As the body count climbs, Kaila needs to stop the killer before she's facing the wrong side of the flames.

THANK YOU
FOR READING!
I WOULD APPRECIATE IT SO MUCH IF YOU LEFT A REVIEW ON AMAZON.

www.ingramcontent.com/pod-product-compliance
Lightning Source LLC
Chambersburg PA
CBHW020606260626
47157CB00003B/882